"He's receiving the Lord," said the man in the Dixie flag T-shirt, calmly. "He'll be fine in a minute."

But Reverend Muldaur wouldn't be fine in a minute. His attempts at breathing were loud and frightening. He was bug-eyed, flailing tongue, wriggling eyebrows. He was spit, snot, urine, feces. He was crying, cursing, keening. He was dancing, heaving, pounding.

"The Lord comes to us in many strange ways," said the Dixie flag T-shirt man. He was as beatific as ever.

And then I realized something.

The only thing more terrifying than watching Muldaur throwing himself voodoo-crazed all over the floor of the platform was watching him lie there absolutely still.

Which is what he was doing now.

And it didn't take me long, worldly gadabout-philosopher and Hemingway sort of guy that I am, to realize what this meant.

Muldaur was dead.

★

PRAISE FOR ED GORMAN'S
SAM McCAIN MYSTERIES

"No writer captures the mood of 1950s middle America...better than Gorman."
—*Ellery Queen Mystery Magazine*

"In Black River Falls...good and evil clash with the same heartbreaking results as they have in the more urban crime drama of Block or Leonard."
—*Booklist*

ED GORMAN

SAVE THE LAST DANCE FOR ME

W✺RLDWIDE®

TORONTO • NEW YORK • LONDON
AMSTERDAM • PARIS • SYDNEY • HAMBURG
STOCKHOLM • ATHENS • TOKYO • MILAN
MADRID • WARSAW • BUDAPEST • AUCKLAND

For Joe and Mitsue Gorman and the grandkids
Shannon, P.J., and Regan
and
For Sadao, Norika, and Hisami Sugiyama
with great love, affection, and joy.

SAVE THE LAST DANCE FOR ME

A Worldwide Mystery/July 2003

First published by Carroll & Graf Publishers.

ISBN 0-373-26461-5

Printed in U.S.A.

I have drawn extensively from Richard Hofstadter's fine book *Anti-Intellectualism in American Life*.
—E.G.

"It was not until I was 8 years old that I discovered that not all the world was Roman Catholic. When John F. Kennedy ran for president, it became clear that many Americans outside our homogeneous enclave considered our faith strange and suspicious and threatening. It turned out that we were a they."
—Anna Quindlen

PART I

ONE

"YOU HEAR THEM, McCAIN?"

"Oh, I hear them all right."

And I did. How could you *not* hear them?

"So you know what they are?" she said.

"You bet I do," I said.

"And you're not scared?"

"Who said I wasn't scared?"

"You did. On the way over."

"Oh."

"So you *are* scared?" she said.

"A little, I guess."

"I'm scared. But then I'm a girl. I'm not a big brave five-foot-four he-man like you."

"Five-five."

"Yeah, in motorcycle boots maybe."

"In motorcycle boots I'd be five-six. If I owned a pair."

"Have I ever told you I'm five-foot-seven?"

"Not more than 4,732 times," I said.

"Almost five-eight, actually."

"All right, I'm scared. Does that make you feel better?"

She gave me her best kid-sister grin and squeezed my hand. It was a kid-sister squeeze, too. Nothing romantic. "Actually, that does make me feel better, McCain. So let's go in, all right?"

Just as we walked away from my '57 red Ford ragtop, she stopped me and said. "Actually, maybe we're imagining it."

"Imagining what?"

"You know. Hearing the rattlesnakes. I don't think you can hear rattlesnakes this far away."

"You want to get out a tape measure?"

The grin again. It always made me want to kiss her. But she was married and we were both reasonably honorable people. So I knew better than to try and she knew better than to let me should I be foolish enough to try.

I guess I should do a little scene-setting here.

The date is August 19, 1960. The town is Black River Falls, Iowa, pop. 20,300. The pretty, red-haired young woman I'm with is Kylie Burke, ace reporter for *The Black River Falls Clarion.* Only reporter, actually. She isn't writing the story—her boss is doing that—but she thought it'd look good on her resume (in case the *New York Times* calls someday) to say she did background on a group of Ozark folks who moved here after getting kicked out of every state contiguous to ours. Seems these folk incorporate rattlesnakes in their services and that is a violation of the law. And after all the rain we had this past spring, there are plenty of timber rattlers to be had in the woods.

Kylie's a bit uneasy about visiting these folks, as am I, so we're here together.

My name is Sam McCain. I'm the youngest and poorest attorney in town. I'm also an investigator for Judge Esme Anne Whitney, the handsome, middle-aged woman who presides over district court. At the age of twenty-four, I earn more from Judge Whitney than I do from my law practice. I'm here tonight because I was summoned by Reverend John Muldaur, the hill-country man who procures the rattlers and oversees the services.

The place we're about to enter is a deserted four-bay service garage that was once part of a Chevrolet dealership on the north edge of town. It's closed up tight except two of the front windows have been smashed and are now filled only with cardboard, so you can hear everything going on. A tornado came through here in '54 and killed eight of us, including a two-month-old, and wiped out everything in this area, including the gleaming new Chevrolet showroom, except the garage. The dealer decided to rebuild on the opposite end of town, apparently figuring his luck might be better come the next tornado.

The cars and panel trucks and pickup trucks parked in the melancholy twilight looked as if they'd been driven across a time warp from the Dust Bowl. Hadn't been washed in years. Had smashed windshields. Cracked headlights. Missing taillights. Tires that held varying amounts of air, some of them nearly flat. Were rusted out so badly the rust had turned into holes in places. And were covered with stickers of all sizes and all lurid colors exhorting pagans to hand themselves over to God and be damned quick about it before it was too late.

The service was just now starting. An Old Testament voice said into a screeching microphone, "Let us now praise the Lord in song."

And that's when we knew that we really had been hearing rattlesnakes. Because as a lone, lame electric guitar began to play "I Know The Bible's Right—

Somebody's Wrong'' the faint rattling sound disappeared.

The man appeared from inside the small door in the
face of the whitewashed concrete-block building. He
was big and wide in his greasy gray work clothes. The
dour line of his mouth exploded into a smile as he said,
"The Lord welcomes you." But the close, hard way
he looked at us made me wonder about his words.

Kylie and I glanced at each other and nodded, and
he widened the doorway by standing aside for us.

Right inside the door we saw the snakes.

A small, wood-framed cage of them sat on a table
with a large crude painting of Christ that was as spooky
as the snakes. He had the demonic visage normally
associated with Satan. On the left side of the table was
a stack of pamphlets with a headline reading: The Jews
Behind John F. Kennedy. You could pretty much guess
what that one was all about. The pamphlets were well
printed on a semi-glossy stock. I wondered where Muldaur had gotten the money for them.

There were no pews, just wobbly folding chairs; no
decorations but an elevated platform holding a lectern,
and four more folding chairs, pushed back against the
wall. You could still smell gasoline and car oil all these
years later, though all the hydraulic lifts had been taken
out and the work pits filled in with concrete.

"Say hello to some new friends!" John Muldaur
shouted into the microphone. He'd been singing in a
sturdy baritone. He kept grabbing a bottle of Pepsi,
gripping it hard as if it was slipping, and guzzling it
down between lyrics.

When they turned around and looked at us, the
twenty or so people filling the folding chairs, I saw
faces that were almost cartoons of joy and grief and

fear and hope as they sang out, immigrant faces
scrubbed clean for churchgoing, unlovely faces for the
most part, mountain people of the deep South who'd
trekked up to the Midwest several generations ago but
had never fundamentally changed, a problem for cops,
social workers, doctors, clerics, and neighbors. Some
of these people still clung to the precepts of "granny
medicine," where you cure lockjaw by crushing a
cockroach in a cup of boiling water and drinking it
down, and staunch the bleeding of a wound by rubbing
chewing tobacco on it. You can't estimate the effects
of poverty on generation after generation of people,
that sadness and despair and madness that so quietly
but irrevocably shapes their thoughts and taints their
souls.

The Muldaurs lived off by themselves, a good half-
mile from the others, who lived in trailers and shacks
in an area called The Corners and mostly worked for
large tenant farms. Ten, twelve families that crossbred
with alarming regularity. The women mostly wore
faded housedresses, their hair beribboned for church.
The men mostly wore threadbare white shirts with the
sleeves rolled up. A couple of them bore dark neckties.
There were six or seven very young children who wore
shorts and shirts because of the eighty-degree heat.
There was a certain apprehension in the eyes of the
young ones. They had not yet been fortified with the
certainty of their elders—that those who did not practice the ways of their faith would perish in hell, and
that all strangers meant you harm. Especially, according to the pamphlets Muldaur had been circulating in
town, the Jews and Catholics all huddled behind Jack
Kennedy in this fall's election. And of course it was

the diabolical Jews stirring up all the trouble down South with the "coloreds."

Naturally, I had mixed feelings about these people. About the only good thing I could say for their religion was that they didn't wear hats of any kind. I've often wondered if God wears a fedora. I mean, have you ever noticed that about religions, their thing for hats? But the rattlesnakes kind of balanced things back in the other direction. The priests and monsignors I grew up with all wore various liturgical hats, caps, and beanies, but one thing you could say in their favor was that they never brought any rattlesnakes to mass, God love 'em. If they had any rattlesnakes, they kept them in the privacy of the rectory and didn't tell us about it.

But then there was the sadness of these people. Not even Steinbeck had gotten to it. The Okies were just displaced farmers who wanted to work and prosper. I never read anything about Okies and rattlers. Dreiser kinda got to these people, I guess. That opening scene of *An American Tragedy* where the family is there on that twilight street corner. I could see these people on that same corner, snakes and all. They were the lost ones and didn't even know it. Few of them would have indoor plumbing; some of them wouldn't even have electricity. A good number of them would die young because they didn't see doctors. And they would spend too much of their time fearing a Jesus who was a parody of the man or god who lived not quite 2,000 years ago. In their version, He despised them and they were appreciative of that fact. It gave some explanation, I suppose, for their smashed and shabby lives.

The singing continued even though John Muldaur set down his microphone and suddenly walked down the aisle between the folding chairs. By this time, his

entire upper body glistened with sweat and he was
muttering some kind of prayer to himself in the sort of
hypnotic fashion people speaking in tongues get into.

No doubt about where he was going, what he was
doing.

He swooped up the two cages of snakes and trans-
ported them back to the makeshift altar. The air
changed. Not just because of the hissing and the rattling. Because of the excitement. I'd never been to an
orgy before but I was sure at one now.

Kylie nudged me. Whispered, "This is scary."

I knew what she meant. There was a sense of violence in the orgiastic response to the snakes. Women
moaned in sexual ways; men stared as if transfixed.
The children looked confused but excited and afraid,
their tiny faces darting up to survey the faces of their
parents, wanting some sort of verbal explanation.

Muldaur reached out his hands. His wife, Viola, took
his left one; his teenage daughter, Ella, his right. Both
were buxom, frizzy-haired, and aggrieved-looking.
They looked as troubled and angry as the rattlesnakes.
All three Muldaurs raised their locked hands and said
a brief prayer. "That I am pure of soul, I have no
doubt, my Lord. Bless me in my purity, Father. Bless
me."

Muldaur dropped the women's hands and turned to
the snakes once again. A collective emotional upheaval
rumbled through the church. The big moment was ap-
proaching. The electric guitar played quick, exotic,
crazed, off-key riffs. Moans; shouts; cries. The snakes
were coming. Orgasm.

My body spasmed when he reached into the cage
and brought forth snake number one. Now slow down
and think about this: You have a small cage containing

four or five poisonous snakes, all right? So what do you do? You just plunge your hand in the open lid up top and grab one of the buggers? Aren't you risking being attacked by one if not more of the snakes in the cage?

But if he was afraid—or even hesitant—he sure didn't show it.

"God has sent us the serpent to reveal our true nature," Muldaur said. Or intoned, I guess. The rattler had brought out his intoning side. "Who wants his soul judged by the serpent?"

This part, I suppose, you're familiar with. You go up there—you, not me—and let the good Reverend Muldaur hand you off the rattler. Then you proceed to grasp it while all the time trying to keep it from biting you. If you manage to hold it for a minute or two without being bitten, that means that your soul is pure and you're one of the chosen. If the snake bites you, you're a sinner whose sins must be redressed. Right after they rush you to the hospital.

Two men and a woman went up and it was about what you might expect. There was a lot of Bible-quoting and a lot of prayer-shouting and one very tiny little girl crying. The snakes scared her. What an irrational reaction. Timber rattlers, in case you don't know, usually have black or dark brown crossbands on a yellow or tan body. The head is yellowish and unmarked. Every once in a while you find one that's black, misleading you into thinking you've got a river rattler, as they're called hereabouts. Makes no difference. Timber rattler or river rattler, you really shouldn't treat them like toys.

The last adult to handle a snake—a heavyset bald man with a milky blue left eye—took on two snakes.

He slung them over his shoulders, he let one wrap about half its body around his neck, and he shook one so furiously that the thing went into snake psychosis.

Then the two men and the woman stood as a group below the lectern and let the congregation touch them, as if they were anointed figures with divine powers. Singing all the time. Everybody was singing. I'm not sure, but I think that even the snakes were singing. True, these people didn't wear hats, but they did sing their collective asses off. The serpents had not bitten these three and so the trio had proved its godliness and what better way to celebrate than with a slightly off-key electric guitar and twenty-some people (and some snakes) joining in congregational song.

I wondered if the ceremony was over. In a Catholic mass everything depends on the sermon. If the sermon's short, you're home free. A short sermon, you can be out of mass in twenty-five minutes flat. I once got an eighteen-minute mass, in fact, leading to my belief that the priest had the trots and needed to get back to the rectory quickly. But God help you if you get the trembling old monsignor. With him, you should pack a lunch.

I had the same feeling here. The snake stuff hadn't taken so long—or been all that terrible, since nobody'd been bitten—so maybe Muldaur wasn't as far gone as I'd feared.

Then the little girl went up and stood next to Muldaur.

She was skinny, pigtailed, terrified. She wore white walking shorts and a blue sleeveless blouse. She looked to be about seven.

"Satan hides even in the hearts and souls of children," Muldaur said.

And the congregation answered him variously with "Yes, Brother" and "The Lord is the Light" and "I do not fear the darkness."

And it all changed for me. This whole experience. Until now a part of me was thinking about how I'd tell my friends about this little adventure. It'd be fun. There'd be a few shivers and a lot of laughs and the comforting knowledge that there really were people crazier than us, after all.

But I hadn't counted on a child handling a snake.

That orgiastic sense only increased. A low, steady murmur of prayer and excitement and fear; women moaning, clutching their breasts almost sexually; men's eyes gleaming with foreboding and sinister anticipation.

"I'm going up there," I said.

Of all the whispers and rumors these people inspired, this was the most disturbing, that they forced children to handle the rattlers. This was the particular reason why state, county, and local officials were always trying to stop them from holding these services. But nobody knew if they actually involved their children or not. Until now.

"Be careful," Kylie whispered.

She didn't try to stop me. She wanted me to go up there.

I started to step into the aisle when I felt something cold and metal pressing against the back of my neck. I'm not a gun guy. But I've read an awful lot of Richard S. Prather paperbacks and so I recognize the feel of a shotgun barrel.

"Just stay right where you are," said the giant who'd let us in. He poked me with the barrel for emphasis.

"God, look at her," Kylie said, loudly enough for people to hear and turn to glare at her.

"Mom!" the little girl shouted. "Please don't make me do this!"

They tell you snakes don't smell. And that they're not cold to the touch. And that they're not slimy. In an objective sense, I knew all this to be true. But I had the sudden visceral feeling that I was in a cave of reeking, slithering, cold-bodied snakes that dripped poison even from their vile scaly bodies.

"Please, Kathryn, help this young girl," Muldaur intoned. "We're trying to conduct a service for the Lord here. He is not kind to those who defy Him."

The young woman, scrawny and pigtailed as her daughter, left her folding chair and ascended to the raised platform. The girl clung to her, throwing her arms around her mother's waist and clutching her the way people clutch life preservers.

"If she will not hold the serpent," Muldaur said, "that means she knows the serpent is already in her heart."

Kathryn bent down and talked to her daughter in a low voice.

Muldaur addressed the congregation. "Pray for little sister Claudia that she might receive the divine courage she needs to do her duty for a loving God."

And they broke into loud, ragged prayer, mother and daughter still talking in low tones back and forth. Mother walked daughter a few steps closer to the snake cages and pointed to the snakes inside as if they were gentle creatures that would be fun to play with.

Claudia was calmer now, snuffling up her tears, standing little-girl tall and little-girl brave. Her mother dabbed at one of Claudia's tears with her finger. Then Mom nodded to Muldaur.

"Unto the Lord will the true heart deliver us," Muldaur said to the congregation as he opened the lid of the second cage. Once again I was startled by the way, almost without looking, he shoved his hand deep into the middle of the piled, hissing rattlesnakes and plucked one out.

He did not pause.

He handed it straight to the little girl.

And that was when the timber rattler, a sort of baby version, much smaller than the previous snakes, used the occasion to lunge at her, striking her right on the cheek.

The little girl screamed. And so, I think, did I.

TWO

"GOD, MR. C, YOU'LL NEVER believe who's pulling up in the parking lot."

Someday, or so one hopes, Jamie Newton, seventeen, sexy, freckled, cute, will learn that "Mr. C" only works with Perry Como on his TV show because his last name happens to begin with C. My name, using that TV style, would be Mr. M for McCain.

But that is only one of many things that has thus far eluded the elusive sweater girl who makes my middle-aged clients make terrible fools of themselves. They find excuses to hang around my office like it's the beer tent on a scorching day at the state fair. It doesn't help that Jamie always looks like all the bad girls you see on the covers of Gold Medal novels about jailbait girls who lead middle-aged men to Death Row.

Jamie also can't answer the phone ("Uh, hello?"), type (my name usually gets typed as "MCCain"; or, on especially bad days, "Mr. C"), buy office supplies ("I just thought pink typing paper would kinda brighten things up"), or resist the call of romance (her boyfriend, Turk, usually calls here four times per her two-hour after-school sessions), or keep her bathroom visits brief ("I guess I've just got a weak liver").

How, you may ponder, did such an unpolished gem come to reside in my cramped little office, itself stuck in the back of a large building that keeps changing businesses?

Small-city lawyers are like small-city bankers. We get paid in a variety of ways. I once got a side of beef for handling a divorce; and a used TV, which I still watch at home, for a traffic case.

I got Jamie from her father, Lloyd, who couldn't afford to pay me for an insurance case I handled for him. In exchange, he said, I'd get his daughter for an unspecified time as my secretary. I'd tried to give her back many times but so far had had no luck. "Nobody deserves her more than you do, Sam," Lloyd always says when I tell him I can't possibly continue to accept his largesse. Lately, I've begun to wonder exactly how he means.

This was two days before my appearance at John Muldaur's church.

Jamie said, "He's the snake guy. Turk'n some of his friends snuck in there one night. Turk says he heard some of them can turn themselves into snakes, like that girl in that movie at the drive-in a couple of summers ago? Did you ever see that one?"

"I think so."

"I just don't know how you could shrink yourself down into a snake."

One of the questions Aristotle no doubt asked himself many times.

"I wonder what he wants, Mr. C."

Came a knock.

"I guess we're about to find out."

She looked spooked. "God, Mr. C, I just thought of something." Stage-whisper.

"What?"

"What if he brought a snake with him?"

"He doesn't carry snakes around with him."

"Well, maybe he can turn himself *into* a snake like that woman did in that movie."

I sighed. "Just answer the door, please, all right?"

"I'm just trying to be helpful is all, Mr. C."

"I appreciate it, Jamie. But please just get the door."

My office is one room. I got all the furniture at various county condemnations, mostly businesses that couldn't pay their taxes. Nothing quite matches but it's all serviceable enough, I suppose. If you can overlook various dings, scratches, scrapes, and gouges. The books on the top two shelves of the bookcase are fine, imposing volumes dedicated to law. The bottom two shelves, hidden somewhat by my desk, run to hard-bound novels and short-story collections. They get read a lot more than the law books.

I always kind of pose when people come in. I place myself behind my desk, put on a pair of reading glasses I got for fifty-nine cents at Woolworths, and pretend to be lost in my perusal of legal documents. "Torts, torts, torts," I've been known to mutter, just loudly enough for my hopefully impressed client to hear.

Jamie opened the door.

Muldaur stood there in a faded work shirt and even more faded work pants. His thick, dark hair spilled over his forehead Elvis-style and his messianic eyes reflected both anger and fear. Oh, yes, I suppose, I should mention the pistol he was holding. It was the kind of handgun my grandfather had, some kind of Colt.

"If this is a stickup," I said, "you've come to the wrong place. I've got exactly thirty-five cents and I'm

planning to blow that on a soda when I get done working.''

''Turk gave me five dollars for my birthday,'' Jamie
said. ''But I already spent it on a pair of shoes.''

He remained in the doorway, huge and fierce. ''I
brought the gun so you'd take me seriously.''

''And why wouldn't I take you seriously?''

''Because nobody else in this town does. They all
think I'm kooky.''

''Kooky,'' if you'll recall, is the word of choice for
Edd Byrnes, the male beefcake on ''77 Sunset Strip,''
one of those realistic TV crime dramas in which the
private eyes all drive Thunderbirds and sleep with vir-
gins. The word is irritating enough when the untalented
Edd Byrnes says it; coming from a crazed and chiseled
Old Testament madman like Muldaur, it was downright comic.

''Why don't you come in and have some coffee and
give your hand a rest? That gun looks pretty heavy.''

''I can make some coffee,'' Jamie said.

She had apparently forgotten the day I pulled an
exceptionally long afternoon in court. Turk stopped by
and they got to necking and everything—I didn't ask
her to detail ''and everything'' when I grilled her later
on—and wouldn't you know it, somehow she forgot
to check the coffeepot and the darned thing caught fire
and gutted the pot so that I had to throw it away and
buy a new one. I hadn't gotten around to replacing the
coffeepot since. The thing was, the burned-up coffee
probably didn't taste a whole lot worse than Jamie's
regular fare.

''That's all right, Jamie. Why don't you just run
over to Rexall and buy us each a cup?''

''Gee, Mr. C, I thought you only had thirty-five cents.''

''Just tell them I'll pay them later this afternoon.''

''Wow, you have a charge account there? That's cool.''

Bliss comes easily to Jamie.

I watched Muldaur watching her as she disappeared out the front door in her tight blue skirt and even tighter summer-weight sweater, black-and-white saddle shoes with tiny buckles in back, bobby sox with discreet hearts on their sides. Wrapped around Turk's class ring (from reform school, presumably) there was enough angora to knit a good-size sweater. She couldn't tell you who John Foster Dulles was or what some guy named Khrushchev did, exactly. But she was well aware of her own considerable charms. Turk, whom I'd never had the displeasure of meeting, was a lucky kid.

''Nice,'' I said.

''What?'' Muldaur whipped around as if I'd poked him with a sharp stick.

''She's a nice-looking young girl.''

''I didn't notice.''

''I noticed that you didn't notice.''

He shoved his craggy face forward. ''If I put a serpent in your hand, would it find you innocent or guilty of lust?''

I smiled. ''Guilty.''

''Well, it wouldn't find *me* guilty. I have cleansed my soul of fleshly pleasures.''

What was the point of pushing further? He'd taken more than a passing interest in Jamie's shapely backside, but why argue about it?

''How may I help you, Reverend?''

"Somebody's trying to kill me."

"If that's true, you should go to the police."

"If you mean that fool Cliffie Sykes, Jr., I told him about it and he said he didn't blame them. I'm being followed. I can feel it, sense it. Somebody took a shot at me as I was leaving the church. Can you believe that? He's supposed to be a lawman."

"Any idea who might be trying to kill you?"

"You believe me, then?"

"I believe that you believe somebody is trying to kill you. So I'd like to hear you explain things a little more."

"I appreciate that." Then, "I think it's the Catholics."

"Ah," I said. "The Catholics. I see."

"And the Jews."

"Ah," I said. "The Jews." Then, "Well, speaking as a Catholic myself, Reverend Muldaur, I doubt the Catholics I know would do such a thing, despite all the really vile things you've said about us. And as for Jews, there're only a few Jewish people in town, and they're just too nice to go around killing people. Or even threatening it."

He watched me. "You're a dupe."

"A dupe of whose, Reverend Muldaur?"

"The pope."

"Ah, a papist dupe."

"You think this is funny?"

"No, what I think this is, is pathetic. You and your people are angry because a Roman Catholic may become president. I hope he does. I plan to vote for him."

"And you know how he'll get in?"

"How?"

"The Jews and their money."

"I hate to say this but my people haven't ever treated the Jews very well. In fact, we've treated them very badly. Even murdered them. And refused to help them during WWII. So why would the Jews and the Catholics be working together, exactly?"

He leaned back. For the first time, he smiled. His smile was even scarier than his scowl. "You ever looked in the basement of your Catholic church?"

I returned his smile. "Now that's always been one of the dumbest conspiracy theories I've ever heard."

"You don't believe it?"

"Of course I don't believe it. I was an altar boy. I was in the church basement hundreds of times."

"You ever hear of subbasements, Mr. McCain?"

"Oh, the old *sub* basement routine, eh?"

"You find the subbasement and you'll find the guns."

It was an old theory often expressed on right-wing radio out here in the boonies. The international cabal of The Jews (note the capital letters) use the basements of Catholic churches to store their weapons. What weapons and for what reason? Because when the revolution comes The Jews and The Catholics, who have only been pretending to disagree at times, will then rise up and impose a One World government on all right-thinking non-Jews and non-Catholics.

I leaned forward on my elbows. "I'm afraid I can't help you."

"You're just like the others, aren't you?"

"First of all, Reverend Muldaur, I'm a lawyer. I'm not a bodyguard."

"You're also a private investigator."

"True."

"So I'd like you to come to one of my services and just look around."

"Look around for what?"

"Somebody who doesn't seem to belong."

"A spy?"

"Something like that. Dupes like you may not realize this, Mr. McCain, but the pope has his own assassins."

"I see. And the first place these assassins would think of is Black River Falls, Iowa?"

"Catholics aren't known for clear thinking. All that mumbo jumbo they believe."

I realized then that the only way I was ever going to get rid of him was to agree to help him. Besides, the service would probably be worth seeing. Much as I feared snakes, there'd be a certain repellent majesty to watching all the snake-handlers do their work.

"What time does it start?" I said.

He didn't have a chance to answer. Jamie was back.

She should have asked for a sack. Instead she gripped the three soggy-hot cardboard containers in her hands. And as she approached the front of the desk where we sat, I saw what was about to happen. She stubbed the toe of her shoe against something and lurched forward. And in lurching forward the coffee went slamming down against the desk.

"Oh, shit!" she cried as the containers exploded, spraying coffee everywhere.

Muldaur leaped from his chair, avoiding the worst of the flying coffee. I didn't do too badly, either, just got a shot of it on my right sleeve. My desk was the main casualty, papers soaked, coffee dripping off the desk edges.

"You let her talk that way?" Muldaur intoned.

"Talk what way?" I didn't know what he was referring to. I was too busy assessing the damage.

"I used the word 'shit,' Mr. C."

"She did it again," he said.

"I was just saying what I said is all," she said miserably.

"Please go get some rags and start cleaning this up, Jamie."

"I'm sorry I used the S word, Reverend," Jamie said earnestly, and I felt sorry for her. She looked very sweet right now. Too bad Muldaur couldn't appreciate her particular form of innocence.

"You wouldn't be using words like that if you came to my church, I can tell you that."

She glanced at me. Scared. She was probably thinking he was going to turn her into a serpent or something. She rushed from the room.

"Two nights from now," Muldaur said. "Eight o'clock. I'm sure you know where it is, the way everybody makes fun of us."

"Strictly speaking, you're breaking the law, Reverend. Bringing poisonous reptiles to a public place."

"Your law," Muldaur reminded me. "Not God's law."

That's one thing I have against organized religions of all kinds. They have all of the answers and none of the questions.

THREE

I GUESS KYLIE AND I were sitting at the wrong angle. From our folding chairs in the back of the place, it sure looked as if the little girl had been bitten by the striking snake. Later on, we'd learn that she'd flung the baby rattler away from her before it could do any damage.

What we didn't mistake was what then happened to Reverend John Muldaur. At the same time the little girl was screaming and holding her hands out for her mommy, Muldaur went into the kind of convulsions Jerry Lewis goes into for laughs. But you could tell by the abrupt mask-like stiffening of his face, which was an expression of shock and horror, that whatever was wrong with him was for real.

His body went into spasms, an arm kicking out, a leg collapsing, the other arm flailing away from his body as if it wanted to tear free.

While one of the male members of the church collected the rattlesnake and put it back in its cage, the other members of the church formed a circle around the minister, who was now flat on his back on the platform, arching up every few seconds to allow his entire body to jerk and twist and convulse. We were part of the circle.

Prayers went up like flares; sobs exploded. A lone

woman hurried-pushed-paddled the children out the door.

An older man in a T-shirt with a Dixie flag on it knelt next to Muldaur saying the same thing over and over, "You're receiving the spirit of the Lord, Reverend, and you shouldn't be afraid."

Some spirit. Some Lord.

"Is there a phone in here?" Kylie asked.

"A phone in the house of the Lord?" a woman snapped back.

"There's a pay phone down the road," one of the more sensible women said.

"He's receiving the Lord," said the man in the Dixie flag T-shirt, calmly. "He'll be fine in a minute."

But Muldaur wouldn't be fine in a minute. His attempts at breathing were loud and frightening. I'd visited my granddad, a "lunger," on a VA ward one time. He'd never recovered from the various lung ailments he'd picked up from various poison gases in WWI. He was like a sea creature writhing on a beach beneath a pitiless sun. My mom always cried for days after seeing him like that.

Muldaur's death—I had no doubt he was passing over—was far noisier and gaudier.

He was bug-eyed, flailing tongue, wriggling eyebrows. He was spit, snot, urine, feces. He was crying, cursing, keening. He was dancing, heaving, pounding.

"The Lord comes to us in many strange ways," said the Dixie T-shirt man. He was as beatific as ever.

"Marv, you've got a motorcycle," the man who'd recovered the baby rattler said. "Run down and call for an ambulance."

Marv trotted out the door.

There are significant moments that you can't quite

deal with completely—they'd explode your mind if you gave yourself to them completely—so a portion of your brain observes you observing the moment. It was like that the first time I ever had sex. I was enjoying it all so much I was afraid I'd start acting real immature and yell stuff or act unlike the sophisticated, jaded sixteen-year-old I was. So a sliver of my mind detached and took an overview of everything. While my body was completely given over to trying to last at least three minutes, my mind was congratulating my body. *You're a man now, young McCain. A worldly gad-about-philosopher stuck in a town where the new co-op grain silo is still a newsworthy event. You, McCain, are a Hemingway sort of guy.*

I was hoping a portion of my mind would detach now and watch me watch Muldaur die. But it didn't. And so all I could do was stand there and hope that there was a life afterward because if this kind of suffering had no meaning—six million Jews in the concentration camps; millions who could be snuffed out with a brief exchange of atomic bombs—then none of the words our religions spoke were anything more than ways of hiding the meaninglessness of everything. And frankly, cosmic meaninglessness scares the shit out of me the way nothing else comes close to. I should never have taken those philosophy courses as an undergrad.

And then I realized something.

The only thing more terrifying than watching Muldaur throwing himself voodoo-crazed all over the floor of the platform was watching him lie there absolutely still.

Which is what he was doing now.

And it didn't take me long, worldly gadabout-

philosopher and Hemingway sort of guy that I am, to
realize what this meant.

Muldaur was dead.

"WHAT'D HE DO? Crap his pants? God, that smell is
awful. I knew those damn snakes would kill somebody
eventually." We were still inside the church. Sykes'd
shooed a lot of the worshipers outside.

With his usual dignity and professionalism, Cliffie
Sykes, Jr., hitched up his holstered Colt .45, hitched
up the Bowie knife he carries in a belt scabbard,
touched a tip of his black Western boot to the corpse,
and screwed up his face into a parody of Porky Pig,
no personal offense meant to you, Porky.

Cliffie, Jr., is the chief of police. At one time Black
River Falls was owned and operated by the Whitney
family, a branch of Eastern millionaires who came out
here when one of the men got involved in some kind
of legal trouble involving stock swindles. They tried to
create a small version of a New England town out here
on the prairie. They were imperious, of course, and
snobs, of course, and contemptuous of the rest of the
town, of course. But they brought sound town government, good and fair law, and an eagerness to keep the
town clean and modern, all the virtues of New England
Yankees.

World War II changed all this, as it changed so
many things, good and bad. Cliff Sykes, Sr., owned a
small construction company at the start of the war.
Then he entered into various federal contracts with the
government. He built airplane runways, roads, training
camps. And his brothers and sisters practiced every
kind of black-marketing there was. One of his sisters
was even an Allotment Annie, a woman so-called be-

cause she married soldiers just about to ship overseas
and collected their monthly allotment checks. One
New York woman was indicted for having forty-six
husbands. I doubt that Helga Sykes had had that many
husbands, only because there weren't that many blind
soldiers.

Anyway, the long run of the Whitney family, begun
in the previous century, came to an end. The Sykes
clan were not only wealthier, they were more powerful.
They took over this part of the state, including our
town. And thus it was that Cliffie Sykes, Jr., who had
failed to pass the police entrance tests given by six
other towns, started his law enforcement career as our
chief of police.

"You smell that, McCain?"

"Yeah, I smell it."

"He crapped his pants."

"Yeah, you said that, Sykes." I only called him
Cliffie when I was so mad I didn't care anymore.

He pointed to the snake cage. "I should go get my
shotgun and kill every one of those bastards." He
pawed his stubby hands on the front of his khaki uniform, the kind Glenn Ford always wears when he's
playing a lawman. Secretly, Cliffie thinks he's Glenn
Ford. Secretly, I think I'm Robert Ryan. Which I am,
pretty much, except for the height, the good looks, the
deep voice, the masculinity, and the charm.

"Or you could always just take them to the woods
and set them free," Kylie said.

He seemed to see her for the first time. She'd be
pretty hard to miss. She was the only pretty one of the
three of us. Everybody else he'd run outside.

"Say, what're you doing here?"

"I'm with McCain."

"And what's McCain doing here, while I'm at it?" he said.

"McCain is doing here what Muldaur asked him to do," I said.

"And that would be what exactly?"

"Exactly, that would be trying to ascertain if somebody was trying to kill him."

"He told you that?"

"He told me that."

"Why'd he think somebody was trying to kill him?"

"He thought it was because of all those pamphlets he was handing out."

"What was wrong with those pamphlets? I read a couple of 'em and they seemed all right to me."

"Why doesn't that surprise me?" I said.

"And anyway, the snakes killed him."

"I don't think so."

"That's what you told me."

"No, it wasn't. That's what you told yourself. You haven't even asked me what killed him."

"Well, if he was doin' all that heebie-jeebies stuff, then what killed him?"

Kylie said, "Poison."

"Yeah, snake poison."

She shook her fetching head. "I don't think so. We studied snakes in biology in college."

"College," Cliffie scoffed. "A training ground for commies."

Kylie sighed. She was used to him. "Snake venom rarely produces symptoms like that."

"Like what?"

"Like what you call the heebie-jeebies."

"So if it wasn't snake poison, what was it?"

"We'll have to let the autopsy tell us," I said.

The ambulance siren cut through our conversation as the boxy white truck swept up in front of the open doorway. You could hear the attendants hitting the ground and yanking the gurney from the back.

Cliffie, thumbs in his gunbelt, swaggered up to meet them.

"Why aren't I surprised Cliffie liked those pamphlets? And I'm not saying that just because I'm Jewish. I'd be mad even if I wasn't." Then she smiled. "And by the way, McCain, the rabbi put some more guns in the basement of your church last night."

"I'll alert the monsignor."

They made swift work of Muldaur, the ambulance boys.

When they were lifting him onto the gurney, Cliffie, ever helpful, said, "Sorry about the smell, boys. He crapped his pants."

"You calling BCI?" I said, referring to the state Bureau of Criminal Investigation. Without their help, small towns just can't do adequate scientific crime investigations.

"For what?"

"For what? To find out who poisoned him."

"Did it ever occur to you, McCain, that maybe one of his snakes bit him earlier and he was just having a delayed reaction. Snakebites can do that, you know."

"Clifford Sykes, Jr., Herpetologist," Kylie said.

"What's that herpe-thing mean?"

"It means snake expert."

"Oh."

He'd obviously thought she'd insulted him. Then he said, "So I call them in and it turns out to be an accidental snakebite and then I look like a fool."

"Gee, I can't imagine you ever looking like a fool, Chief," Kylie said in her sweetest voice.

"Well, God knows you and that left-wing rag you work for have tried to make me *sound* like one every chance you get."

Maybe it was the innumerable times he'd arrested people for crimes they hadn't committed. Maybe it was the year he pocketed half the ticket sales to the policeman's dance. Maybe it was the time *The Clarion* pointed out that it was Cliffie's first cousin Luther who was not only selling our town its police vehicles but also charging twenty percent over the sticker price. It wasn't real hard to make a case against Cliffie.

"We couldn't do it without your help," Kylie said, all sweetness again.

Cliffie was about to respond when one of the children raced into the church. Cliffie did not like this. When Cliffie tells you to stay out, he gets most unpleasant if he sees you defying him.

He lunged for the kid and shouted, "Hey, you, twerp!"

"Maybe he'll shoot him," Kylie said.

"Nah. Nothing worse than a pistol-whipping, probably."

The kid wanted to see the snakes, was the thing. He rushed up to the cage and stood gazing in fear and amazement at the serpents that hissed and rattled at a world as alien to them as theirs was to us.

"You get away from there now," Cliffie said.

"They wouldn't bite me, Chief," the boy said. He was probably eight, with a bowl-job haircut like Larry's of the Three Stooges, something Mom probably gave him at home. "I don't have sin in my heart. I really don't."

"You heard what I said."

Cliffie yanked him down from the platform and dragged him outside.

Something had been troubling Kylie all evening. Something that was becoming clearer and clearer on her girlish, elegant face. Somehow, I sensed that it didn't have anything to do with the church here, frightening as that had been.

"You GIVE ME a ride home, McCain? I guess I've about had it. Watching him die like that took it out of me." She slid her arm through mine. "Let's go outside."

Heat, mosquitoes, fireflies, and the smell of gasoline, cigarettes, and sweaty people awaited us. The place was already becoming a carnival. On a summer night in a small town there's nothing front-porch folks would rather do than follow ambulances. *Put up some iced tea there, honey, and we'll see where that ambulance is goin'. Hurry, now.* More dramatic than TV, cheaper than the movies. And they were just now pulling up, forming a semi-circle around the cars of the church-goers. They were practiced enough at all this to leave plenty of room for the official vehicles to get in and out. And they were bold enough to go right up to Muldaur's flock and ask them questions. They were sure this just had to involve snakes, and what could be more exciting than something that involved snakes *and* was cheaper than going to the movies?

But it wasn't all front-porch types, and that surprised me. Reverend Thomas C. Courtney was there, for one, the first minister to look as if *Esquire* had dressed him. I wondered if the apostles had worn starched blue dress shirts, white ducks, and deck shoes. And driven green

MGs. I always enjoyed driving past his church to see the titles of his forthcoming sermons. ''You, John Paul Sartre, and The Crucifixion'' was still my favorite. We used to parody that title. I came up with ''You, Gabby Hayes, and The Heartbreak of Hemorrhoids.'' (I was reading *Mad* magazine a lot in those days.) Courtney appealed to what we call, out here anyway, the gentry. He'd angered a lot of Catholics lately by preaching a piece written by Dr. Norman Vincent Peale, the most successful Protestant minister of our day, who claimed that Jack Kennedy was, as a Catholic, beholden to Rome and that a vote for Kennedy was thus a vote for papal rule.

Finding Sara Hall here was even more surprising. A fading country-club beauty who'd been to the Mayo Clinic several times for what was locally called ''a little drinking problem,'' Sara was a friend of my employer, Judge Whitney, and a woman I liked. Her hands twitched sometimes, and she was known to have had a couple minor breakdowns in very public places a few years back. One day, seeing me on the street and having met me only once, she asked if I'd have a cup of coffee with her. I was surprised but I went. And when our coffee came and she'd had a couple of swallows, she said, ''I was just afraid I might pop in somewhere and have a drink. But instead I can sit here and talk to you. I really appreciate this.''

Muldaur's people had gathered in front of two battered Chevrolet trucks, from one of which issued the plaintive cry of hill music in its purest form, not steel guitars but slide guitars, the kind of music first heard on these shores a couple hundred years ago when Irishers landed on the shores of the Atlantic. The voices of the girl singers were my favorite parts, high-pitched wails relating tales of doomed lovers and the men who enslaved them. The lyrics were changing now, influencing country music and being influenced by it at the same time. This was the music of a subculture that would never become mainstream. To find life as it was lived a hundred years ago, maybe a hundred and fifty years ago, you didn't have to travel far.

I saw it peripherally, not sure at first that I did see it, the big man who'd guarded the church door leaning over to slap a small woman, hard, across the mouth. This was in the far shadows, beyond the wall of crunched and crushed vehicles they drove. They stood between two such vehicles. They were easy to see.

It was just at that moment that Cliffie starting baying orders for all the people who'd been inside the church to start giving statements to his men—first cousins, second cousins, shirttail cousins—who were now moving among the flock with ball-point pens and nickel back-pocket notebooks. Cliffie had once seen BCI agents do this and had forever after imitated it. Hey, this idea of interviewing witnesses seemed like a pretty neat-o keen idea. Boy, where was this scientific detection stuff going to end, anyway?

"You mind if we leave? I'm getting kind of tired."

Kylie's voice broke somewhere in the middle of that last sentence and then she did something I'd never seen her do before. She started crying. Not hard, not loud, mostly just large, gleaming tears collecting in the corners of her dark eyes. She didn't wait for my answer. "C'mon, McCain, let's go, all right?"

FOUR

IT IS A STRANGE summer for me. The girl I've loved since grade school is in Kansas City, hiding out from the scandal of running off with our town's most important lawyer. Married lawyer, I should add. Two kids and all. Lawyer and wife have made up. The beautiful Pamela Forrest is, however, pretty much gone forever. Mary Travers, the girl I should have fallen in love with—as much as you can determine something like that, I mean—is getting married to the man whose father owns the local Rexall plus a whole lot of other property in the county. She still loves me, or so she said the last time I saw her, but I've screwed up her life too many times as it is.

And the other day I was sitting in the backyard of my folks' place and I started to study them. Not just look at them. Study them. And see how old they're getting. And I felt scared and sad and lonely because they're such good people and I sure don't want them to die. And Mrs. Goldman, my landlady, about whom I've had more than a few erotic fantasies, went to some kind of cancer meeting in Iowa City—her sister recently died of cancer—and she came back with those sticker decals you put on your medicine cabinet mirror, CANCER'S SEVEN DANGER SIGNALS. And put them on every medicine cabinet mirror in the house, including mine. And I started thinking about it. I mean, she meant well. But I started thinking about it. That I could die, too. That it wasn't impossible for a twenty-four-year-old to pass over.

And then at the grocery store last Saturday, everybody crowded in there buying potato chips and beer and Canada Dry mixes for highballs. I saw a lot of the kids I'd graduated with from high school. And they all had wives and kids in tow. And looked happy. And grown up. And I thought of what a mess my life was and how in a lot of ways I was still a kid and sometimes that was all right but other times it made me ashamed of myself. Maybe I'd never be Robert Ryan but at least I could be an adult like my dad. He had to quit school when he was in tenth grade to help support his family. I guess that grows you up pretty fast.

And now here I am with Kylie, whom I have this sort-of stupid half-assed crush on even though she's married and I sure don't want to get involved in anything like that, and we're just riding the prairie night with the top down in my red Ford ragtop, taking the long way home at her request, out on the blacktop that runs between the woods and the river, the moon high and round and silver-gold, and the cattle and the horses lowing in the farmyards, and a lone motorboat out on the river, its wake phosphorescent as it cuts the moonlight, and I'm wondering if Kylie feels as lonely as I do at this moment.

She said, "This feels good."

"Yeah. It does." Though I wasn't quite sure what "it" referred to.

"Everybody should have a convertible."

"Can't disagree with you there."

"Even the pig shit smells sort of good tonight."

"Yeah, I was just thinking that myself. Boy, this pig shit really smells good tonight."

She slugged me on the arm.

She didn't say anything for a time, we were just cruising along the river, and there was this houseboat then and even from here you could hear the Latin music and the people all laughing, and she said, "I wish I was out there."

"On the houseboat?"

"Uh-huh."

"How come?"

"Oh, I've got my reasons."

"What you've got is some sort of secret, don't you?"

She laughed. "Cliffie Sykes, Jr., Herpetologist. Samuel McCain, Mind Reader."

"So you going to tell me what it is?"

"No. Because if I do I'll get sad again. And I don't want to be sad for a while."

"I don't blame you there."

"Sometimes, it feels sorta good to be sad. You know what I mean?"

"I think so."

"But most of the time it just feels like shit to be sad." Then, "Could you turn up that song? I love it."

Fats Domino. "Blueberry Hill."

I GOT HER home about half an hour later.

She lived in a cottage isolated on the edge of a creek and snuggled between elms. There was an old swing set in the side yard. You could almost hear the happy squeals of kids from other times. Every once in a while, tired of newspapering, she'd say, "I should just

pack it in and have some kids, McCain.'' She hadn't
said that for some time.

The house was dark. Her road-weary 1951 Dodge
sat in the grassy drive. Chad's car wasn't there. Chad
taught English at the University of Iowa, forty-five
minutes away. He was one of many grad students there
writing a novel on the side. We'd never cared much
for each other. He was this big, blond guy who dom-
inated every room he was in with his harsh opinions
and uncharitable evaluations of everybody around him.
I think the word I'm struggling for here is jerk. He
caught me reading a Gold Medal paperback by Charles
Williams at the Rexall lunch counter one time and has
ever since called me, with great scorn, ''The Gumshoe.'' I planned to tell him someday that Williams
was a better stylist than he or his fellow wanna-bes
would ever be. But I was waiting till I got my full
growth before I did. He was something like six-two.

''Guess Chad's still in Iowa City, huh?'' I said.

''Yeah,'' she said.

''Probably working on his novel.''

''You know better than that.'' Not looking at me.
Just staring at the dark house.

''I do?''

''You're not exactly an idiot, McCain.''

''I'm not?''

''Chad's got himself a girlfriend.''

''Oh.''

''That's what he's doing in Iowa City.''

''You sure?''

''I skipped work one day and went to Iowa City and
followed him around. She lives off-campus. They spent
all afternoon in her apartment. She's a junior. Really
beautiful.''

"Maybe it's not what you think."

"All afternoon and it's not what I think?"

"So what're you going to do?"

"Kill him is what I should do."

It was a night of fireflies and frogs on the cusp of the creek and boxcars rattling through the darkness up in the hills. The ragtop idled a little rough. Tune-up time.

Then she was up and gone to the dark cottage, cursing when the key didn't open the front door first try, exploding into sobs once she was inside.

I thought of going in after her but she probably wanted to be alone. I liked her and I felt sorry for her. The good ones always get it. Maybe the Reverend Thomas C. Courtney could explain that one in one of his sermons. Why the good ones always get it. Or maybe I could put in a long-distance call for John Paul Sartre and he could tell me.

I went home.

JUDGE WHITNEY CALLED me early the next morning and told me what she wanted. Soon after the call I ate breakfast at Al Monahan's. Al lost both his legs on Guam but the way he gets around in his wheelchair should qualify him for the Indy 500. People, including the wasp Brahmins, started going to Al's out of duty and pity. But they kept coming back because the food's so good. Al and his harried crew have the most successful restaurant in town.

When I got outside on the street again with my toothpick and my Lucky, my easy-over eggs and toast sitting just fine and dandy in my stomach, I saw three middle-aged men standing beside a small black car, assessing it. There'd been an advertising sign for the

Edsel—"Rock and Roll, Sputnik, Flying Saucers, and now the Edsel!"—that had irritated the old-timers. But that was because it reminded them of their age, and seemed to exclude them from driving such a youthmobile.

The Volkswagen this trio was looking at was controversial for another and far more serious reason. Men their age had fought hard to defeat Germany, leaving many of their friends behind on European soil. Now here came the krauts insinuating their way into the American economy with their undersized, underpriced cars that were threatening to displace a segment of the American car market. The fear was that these little cars would ultimately throw a whole lot of American workers out of jobs. I didn't have to stop to hear the dialogue. I knew it by heart. And agreed with it. "This was the car that Hitler had built for his people. They shouldn't be allowed to sell it over here."

I was glad to get into my red Ford and head out to the edge of town. It was a butterfly morning. In places beneath heavy branches the shaded areas still gleamed with dew. All the early-morning kids on their trikes and bikes looked fresh and alert at the top of the day. A skywriting plane was writing "Make it Pepsi!" The radio was wailing a great old Elvis tune "I Want You, I Need You, I Love You." The Church of Elvis. I was a faithful communicant.

I tried not to think about rattlesnakes or Kylie's unfaithful husband or my loneliness. I just tried to enjoy the day, the way all the positive-thinkers like Pat Boone tell you to. His best-seller of advice to high-schoolers "Twixt Twelve & Twenty" had teenagers laughing from coast to coast.

And I did, too, all the way out to the trailer behind

the church where Muldaur had died last night. The exchange of gunfire, however, took the day down a notch. Even Pat Boone would have to admit that gunfire tends to put a pall on a nice day.

Six or seven quick shots burnished the air.

It was a butterfly day out here, too. Except all the butterflies were hiding behind boulders so they wouldn't get hit in all the gunplay.

The first thing that came to mind was the Hatfield-McCoy feud of lie and legend, two hillbilly families that warred with each other generation unto generation. They came to mind because the trailer resembled a shack, patched as it was with cardboard, sheet metal, stucco, anything that could be adhesed, nailed, or otherwise appended to the rusted-out abode. A shotgun poked from its lone front smashed window.

Then there was the motorcycle with a sidecar. A very small man, not much bigger than a munchkin, looking an awful lot like Yosemite Sam with his long red beard and floppy battered hat, crouched behind his cycle, firing away with his shotgun at the trailer. What you have to understand here is that neither party was seriously trying to hit the other. Nobody's aim could be that bad. The sidecar was more interesting than the gunfire. From it stuck the barrels of at least eight or nine long rifles, shotguns, and even—I kid you not, as Jack Paar likes to say—a hunting bow. As in bow and arrow.

The first thing I considered was the health and well-being of my ragtop. I swung back in front of the church and parked it there. Then I snuck around the side where I could be seen and heard. The folks firing the guns were under the impression—probably correct—that out here in the boonies nobody would bother them. Hell, nobody would probably *hear* them.

But being the good-citizen type, I raised my voice and said, "If you people don't put your guns down I'm going to call Sykes and have him come out here."

"Viola! Viola! Who the hell is this guy?" shouted the man with all the weapons.

"He works for Judge Whitney!" a female voice from inside the trailer shouted back.

"Judge Whitney! She's the one threw me in the jug for lumpin' Bonnie up that time!"

"Lumpin'" in mountain language means putting lumps on another person's body.

"We better stop firin', Ned!"

"Put your gun down and walk away from your motorcycle," I said. "With your hands up."

"You ain't even got a gun," he said.

"That's right."

"And you ain't even much bigger'n me, either."

"Right again, pal. But it's me or Cliffie."

He frowned and spat a stream of tobacco that was probably carcinogenic enough to scar the earth forever. "Cliffie. One day me'n that sumbitch is gonna tangle, I'll tell you that."

"Away from the motorcycle. Hands up. Now." I said it just the way Robert Ryan would have.

Cliffie loved beating up people who didn't have the education or the money to fight back legally. A man like this would give Cliffie plenty of thrills.

He moved away from the motorcycle. With his hands up.

"Now, you come out of the trailer," I said.

"With your hands up," Ned said. Then to me,

"I gotta have my hands up, *they* gotta have *their* hands up."

"Fair enough," I said.

There were two of them, mother and daughter, the Muldaurs. They wore the same kind of tent-dresses they'd worn last night, the kind that hides bodies too big, shame dresses really.

"C'mon over here," I said. "I want you folks to tell me what's goin' on."

"I want my money," Ned said.

"What money?"

"Money their mister owed me for snakin'."

"I thought Muldaur did his own snakin'."

"He could handle 'em but he couldn't find 'em. I took him out with me about six months ago and he couldn't find nothin'. Not even a garter snake. Muldaur's the only one made any money that day."

"He paid you what he could," Viola Muldaur said. She had a wide, Slavic face that had likely been pleasant before hard times had taken their toll. It was too easy, what with her snakes and all, to dismiss her as an alien of some kind.

"So he paid you to find them?" I said.

He nodded. If he weighed 120, 100 of it had to be dirt, grime, slime. The ratty red beard had things crawling in it. The gums looked charred—yes, folks, charred—and the one blue glass eye managed to appear goofy and sinister at the same time. He wore a filthy cotton vest with nothing but scrawny, hairless chest beneath, and a pair of Sears Roebuck jeans even more vile than the vest. And no shoes. His toenails had some kind of luminescent green-blue fungus growing on them. I'd be proud to have him in my family.

"He owed me for that last batch."

"And you came here with your shotgun?" I said. "You ever hear of sending somebody a bill?"

"That's how we settled things in the hills."

"He's right, mister," Viola said. "We wouldn't actually hurt nobody. Just make a lot of noise. And what're you doin' out here, anyway?"

"Just wondered if you'd had any ideas about who might've poisoned your husband."

"I sure do," the girl said.

"You hush, Ella."

I studied their eyes. Ella had been crying. Viola was wiping tears from her eyes. Ella seemed unsteady, ready to erupt. Viola looked calm. Different people react differently to the death of a loved one. Still, Viola's reaction made me curious. Ella kept touching a rashed spot just below her knee. She'd rubbed something on it.

"You tellin' me you don't have no money?"

"That's what I'm tellin' you, Ned."

"I suppose they give you credit down at the TV store."

"John hisself bought that set. I don't know nothin' about it."

"I bet."

I said, "You were going to say something, Ella. About who might have killed your father."

"Ella *wasn't* gonna say nothin' and Ella ain't *gonna* say nothin'," Viola said. "You understand that, girl?"

Ella, a whipped dog, nodded slowly. She suddenly seemed winded, washed out. She looked older today, maybe sixteen or seventeen.

"And as for you, mister, I want you off my property."

"You seem to forget your husband hired me."

"Yeah. To find out who wanted to kill him." She smiled with dirty teeth. "And you done a whale of a good job at finding out who, didn't you?"

Ned's whole body did a delightful kind of puppet-dance. "Hee-hee, she sure got you on that one, city boy."

That was probably the first time a man from Black River Falls, Iowa, had ever been called a city boy. In a way, it was flattering.

I glanced back at his junky motorcycle, big-ass old Indian, and the sidecar with all the artillery in it. "You expecting a war any time soon?"

"I sure am, city boy. And when it comes, I'll be ready for it."

I'd suddenly run out of things to say to these people. I felt sorry about leaving Ella behind—she was young enough there might still be hope for her—but there wasn't anything I could do short of kidnapping her. And if I did that, Ned here would probably get out his bow and arrow.

I went around and got in my ragtop.

WHAT EXACTLY, YOU may ask, is the Cincinnati Citadel of Medinomics? Many before you have asked and many after you will do likewise.

As near as I can figure, it's a diploma mill. The "Medi" part I get (medicine), but the "nomics" thing I think they stuck in there just because it sounds sort of vaguely official.

Its most prestigious, and only, local graduate is Doc Novotony, who is yet another relative of Cliffie's. Doc had to battle the state medical board to get his ticket but they finally had to give in after the state supreme court ordered them to. Cliffie, Sr. made Doc the county medical examiner, which was all right with everybody because he did so with the tacit understanding that Doc, who is actually a great guy, would never actually touch a living human being. He would work only on corpses, people figuring how much harm can you do to a stiff? And if he didn't have a stiff to work on, he generally sat in his office in the morgue in the basement of the courthouse, chain-smoked his Chesterfields, gnawed on his Klondike candy bars, read his scandal magazines ("Kim Novak's Naughty Nite Out With The Football Team!"), and avoided damaging his five-six, 220-pound figure by doing any exercise at all.

"Hey," he said when I walked in, his feet up on his desk as usual. It being Saturday morning, his voluptuous middle-aged receptionist Rita, with whom he was or wasn't having an affair, depending on which town gossip you talked to, wasn't here. He wore floppy loafers, red Bermuda shorts, a polo shirt with a Hawkeye insignia on it (he was quoted as saying once that he was neither Jew nor Christian but Hawkeye, meaning a fan of the various University of Iowa Hawkeye teams), and a smile on his face. He almost always looked happy, as if he were spiting the corpses tucked in the drawers all around him.

"Cliffie said you'd be here, McCain, and that I wasn't supposed to tell you anything."

"Good ole Cliffie."

"How come you're interested, anyway?"

I shrugged. "I was out there when he died. Plus I got a phone call."

His blue eyes became downright merry. "Herr Himmler?"

Which is what he called Judge Whitney, my three-quarter-time employer.

"Uh-huh."

"Why would she give a damn about Muldaur?"

"She doesn't. But Richard Nixon's going to swing through here after he stops in Cedar Rapids and she's afraid we'll all look like a bunch of rubes to him if we've got a murder going involving a minister who used snakes in his church. She's going to have dinner with Nixon. Said she doesn't want our little town to sound like a bunch of mountain crackers."

He beamed. "Richard Nixon? Really? I'm gonna vote for him. I guess I've got to give the old broad one thing—she sure is connected."

As she was. In the past few years, she's golfed three or four times with Ike and dined with celebrities as various as Leonard Bernstein, Dinah Shore, and Jackie Gleason; next month she was scheduled to be on the same Chicago dais as Claire Booth Luce and Dr. Joyce Brothers.

"So what's the word on Muldaur?" I said.

He took his feet down. "You want all the mumbo jumbo or English?"

"English will do fine."

"He was poisoned."

One thing about those Cincinnati Citadel of Medinomics graduates—you can't put anything over on them.

"Anything a little more specific?"

"Ah, you do want the mumbo jumbo. I appreciate the opportunity to sound like I know what I'm talking about." He cleared his throat. Pulled up his baggy trousers. The spotlight was his. "Technically, he died from exhaustion."

"Exhaustion? You're kidding. I thought you said he was poisoned."

"He was. Strychnine has that effect. You know all those convulsions he had?"

"God, they were terrible."

"They literally wore him out. Yes, he was poisoned, and that asphyxiated him. But the convulsions were so severe he also had a heart attack brought on by sheer exhaustion."

"God, what a terrible way to go."

"Been better poetic justice if one of his vipers got him. But the vipers wouldn't have done half the damage the poison did."

"But doesn't poison like that taste terrible?"

"Yeah, but the way he worked himself up during those ceremonies... He might have swallowed it and not realized it. He wouldn't have had to drink a whole hell of a lot of it. Cliffie talked to one of the church-goers who said Muldaur was always guzzling Pepsi. Somebody coulda put it in that."

"I need to talk to his wife."

"Cliffie said she wasn't any help."

"Yeah, she probably didn't respond well to when Cliffie clubbed her."

Doc grinned. "I shouldn't put up with you making fun of my beloved cousin that way. Without him I wouldn't be medical examiner of this here county. And I wouldn't be permitted to wear my stethoscope in public, either."

"Now, that would be a shame. You look very good strutting down the street in your stethoscope."

He giggled. "That's what the ladies tell me, counselor."

"Exhaustion, huh," I said, thinking about every-thing he'd told me. Then an image of Muldaur convulsing came to me. Seeing something like that diminished our entire species. I'd always known we were vulnerable. I just didn't like to be reminded of it in such a grotesque fashion.

FIVE

I GUESS I SHOULD explain about our dunking. It's one of our darkest family secrets. Everybody in my family dunks. We dunk doughnuts, we dunk coffee cake, we dunk sandwiches, my kid sister, at least before she moved to Chicago, dunked her French fries in her Pepsi. In moments of great excitement I've been known to dunk a slice of pizza in my glass of beer. Maybe it's genetic. You don't want to know about family reunions, believe me. The inclination to dunk affects multiple generations. Eighty, ninety McCains planted at various picnic tables in a public park. Dunking. All at the same time.

Anyway, after visiting Doc, I stopped over to ask my dad about a guy who used to work at the plant and then all of a sudden there were three of us at the kitchen table, dunking long johns in our coffee.

My dad's three biggest dreams had come true. He produced a kid who became a professional man, he bought a house, and he paid saved-up cash for a 1958 Plymouth that has the fin-length of a shark.

My mom's three biggest dreams have come true, too. My dad returned safely from the war, her sister survived breast cancer, and she finally got the Westinghouse washer-dryer combination she's always wanted, thanks to the way Betty Furness hawks them on TV.

My dad was mid-dunk when I said, "So did Walter ever tell you why he dropped out of Muldaur's church?"

"He sure did."

"How come?"

He held up his finger, meaning please let him finish swallowing. He's a little guy, which is where I get it, and when Mom's in high heels they look sort of funny together, not mother-son but more like big sister-little brother, but when they get out on the dance floor to Benny Goodman, their musical tastes having ossified around 1946, they are dazzling, gray hair, girdle, shoe lifts, bald head, and all.

"Muldaur tried to get frisky with his wife."

"What? You're kidding."

"Oh, no," Mom said. "One of the women at the beauty parlor said that the same thing happened to her daughter-in-law. Apparently, he was a frisky man."

I don't have to tell you what frisky means. Dad rarely uses vulgarities and Mom never does. That particular genetic streak ended with me, I'm afraid.

I wondered if Cliffie knew anything about this. Muldaur was not only a religious bigot but a ladies' man as well. Two motives had already surfaced for his being killed. There would likely be more. There usually are in homicide investigations. You take a guy like Muldaur, you might find six, seven people who'd considered killing him, each with very specific and unique reasons of their own.

Part of my mom's john got soaked and fell in her coffee. She used her spoon to rescue it, then ate it like a piece of cereal. I'm more careful with my dunking.

More timid, I guess. I'm well aware of how pieces get too wet and fall off. I don't want that to happen to me.

"Where'd Walter move to, anyway?"

"Cedar Rapids. Penick & Ford plant. He's got a brother-in-law there who's a big shot in the union."

"He didn't happen to move because of Muldaur, did he?"

"Heck, no. Walter? He knew what he was getting into when he married Jinny."

"What he was getting into? What's that mean?"

"You know," my dad said, as if we were telepaths. "Her, uh, bosoms."

"She had big knockers, as the men like to say," mom said, "your father included."

"Yeah, now that I think about it," I said, "I guess she did."

"Guys were always gettin' frisky with her," Dad said. "Muldaur was just one more. His wife was the one who thought the snake stuff was so neat, anyway. So when she told Walter about Muldaur askin' her to meet him out to the old Tyler farm, he just told her that he didn't ever want her to go back there to church."

"You know who you should talk to," Mom said.

"Who?"

"Kenny Thibodeau."

"You're kidding."

"No. He wrote a long article on Muldaur and his church, back when he worked for *The Clarion*."

Kenny Thibodeau was a local kid who graduated from the University of Iowa journalism school in 1955 or so. He came back to town here, became the assistant editor of the local paper, got himself married, had a son, took up golf, and could even be seen ushering at the Pentecostal church on Saturday morning.

Then he read *On The Road* by Jack Kerouac and claimed to have the same kind of vision St. Paul had on the road to Damascus, or wherever he was going. Well, not exactly the same, of course. Paul claimed to have seen God and renounced all sin. Kenny Thibodeau, on the other hand, claimed to have seen Allen Ginsberg and Neal Cassady. And instead of renouncing sin, he embraced it. All kinds of sin. He left his wife and child and moved to the West Coast. He reappeared a year later, his wife and child long gone, no longer the buttoned-down, crew-cutted Kenny we'd known and ignored. He was a beatnik. I hate that word, it's a press word, but that's what he was. He had the goatee, he had the black horn-rimmed glasses, the black turtleneck, the black chinos, the black socks, and, worst of all, the Jesus sandals. I'm no fashion plate but there's something about socks and sandals that rankles. At least he'd spared us the beret.

Kenny had been coming and going ever since. He went to London, Paris, San Francisco, New York. And always returned. He supported himself by writing pornography, or what the moralists called pornography, anyway. Paperbacks with sexy covers and suggestive titles but virtually nothing explicit inside. *Lesbo Lodge* was one of his, as was *Life of a Lesbo*. Kenny lived in a trailer near the west end of town. We had coffee whenever we ran into each other. I enjoyed him without quite approving of him. And I disapproved of him because I was probably jealous. He traveled, he supported himself writing, albeit somewhat scandalously, and he was always going to Iowa City on the weekends and coming back with wild tales of undergraduate English majors who "know how to swing, man, and I do mean swing."

I'd never thought of asking Kenny for actual hard information. I'd never suspected Kenny of *having* any hard information. But maybe Mom was right. Maybe before he'd taken up marijuana, cheap wine, and Zen there had been an actual fact or two rolling around inside his mind.

"He looks so silly in that goatee," Mom said. "But he's still a nice boy."

Dad laughed. "Don't tell that to Emily at the rectory. She thinks he should be put in jail for writing those dirty books."

"Yeah," I said. "She also was going to start a petition to put D. H. Lawrence in jail until she found out he was dead."

SUMMER SATURDAY MORNINGS in Black River Falls are a good time to be on the streets. The merchants are happy because business is good; the farm wives are happy because they're getting their hair done or buying something new for themselves—it could be a dress or an electric mixer, it doesn't matter, it's just the idea of getting something new; the little ones are happy because there's a triple feature plus a chapter of a serial at the Rialto; the teenage girls are happy because they'll be modeling their swimsuits at the public pool; the teenage boys are happy because they'll get to watch the teenage girls model those swimsuits.

The street rods are out already. They'll go out to the park where the boys will polish them the way pagans used to polish false idols. Chopped and channeled hymns of metal and fiberglass and rubber that wouldn't think of playing Fabian or Frankie Avalon or anybody like that, sticking strictly to Mr. Chuck Berry and Mr. Little Richard and Mr. Gene Vincent and his Blue Caps. There are also "jes' folks" kinds of cars, bicycles, a horse-drawn Amish buggy or two (there's an Amish community twenty miles due east of here), and a whole bunch of motorcycles, most of the riders being Marlon Brando in their minds (but then who do the grandmas riding the big Indians imagine themselves to be?).

Kenny Thibodeau made it easy for me. He was sitting in the town square reading a John Steinbeck paperback, *In Dubious Battle*.

His black uniform was intact. Even his shades were black. The only way I knew he saw me was the way he tilted his head up at me.

"Hey, man."

"Hey, man, yourself, Kenny."

I sat down next to him on the bench.

"How they hangin', man?"

"Oh, you know," I said. I've never known how to answer that particular cliché. They're hangin' low, hangin' high? Which way is best? "How's the writing going?"

"Pretty good. They jumped me up in advances."

Two paperbacks rested on the pigeon-blessed bench between us.

"Take 'em, I was gonna give 'em to you anyway when I ran into you."

I picked them up. The covers were nicely illustrated. One showed a virginal young blonde woman in a matching skirt and sweater and bobby sox and penny loafers staring over her shoulder at a severe but coldly beautiful older woman standing in a shadowed doorway. "*Student Advisor*... Lesbos ruled this campus until a stud professor was hired.'' The other one featured a well-built shirtless young girl in bed with a nearly naked older woman. ''*Sex Machine*... His 'tools of the trade' could turn lesbos into man-lovers.''

''The Nobel Committee wants every copy of those they can find,'' he said.

''Yeah?''

''Yeah,'' he laughed, ''so they can burn 'em.''

''You ever actually meet a lesbian?''

''I heard one on the radio once.''

''How do you know she was a lesbian?''

''She said she was.''

''I guess that's one way of telling.'' Then I said, ''My cousin's a lesbian and she's actually very nice. I mean, nobody in the family wants to acknowledge it but she never even pretends to be interested in guys romantically.''

''Maybe you could introduce me to her sometime. You know, maybe she could teach me how they talk, code words, stuff like that.''

''I think they talk pretty much like everybody else. At least Alison does.''

''You mean Dr. Edmond DeMille wasn't right? They don't have a secret handshake?''

''Who's Dr. Edmond DeMille?''

''I am. That's one of my pen names. I wrote a book called *When Your Daughter Is a Lesbo*. DeMille is even more full of shit than I am.''

That was Kenny's greatest virtue. The self-deprecation. He didn't harangue you the way some of his compatriots did. I'd never even heard him describe anybody as ''square.'' That was why I liked his books, too. I appreciated the errant erections they sometimes inspired but even more I appreciated the humor he was able to sneak in.

"My mom tells me you did an article on Muldaur."

"Yeah," he said. "Hey, wasn't that wild? Him dying and all."

"The judge wants me to find out what happened before Richard Nixon gets here."

He whipped his shades off. "Richard Nixon is coming *here?*"

"That's right. In six days. Having dinner with her at her club."

"That Nazi."

"I agree, Kenny. But right now I need to know about Muldaur. You find out anything interesting about him?"

"Interesting meaning sleazy?"

"Yeah. Something like that."

"He was porking a lot of the ladies in his flocks."

"That I've heard."

"And then about six months ago, he came into some money."

"Inherited, you mean?"

Kenny shook his head. He had beagle brown eyes. Plaintive. He made you want to put a dog biscuit in his paw. "I guess not. He just suddenly had some money. Paid off the loan on that garage he uses for his church. Paid off a lot of bills, too."

"But nobody knows where the money came from?"

"Nobody I talked to."

"Wonder where he'd get money? The place he came from—those hill people don't have any money." He hesitated. "You want me to see what I can find out."

"I'd appreciate it."

"In fact, maybe I can get some ideas from it. You

know, sort of playing private eye. You ever watch 'Peter Gunn?' "

"Never miss it." And I didn't.

"How about that Mancini music?"

Henry Mancini had revolutionized television theme music. His music was as much a part of the noir feel of the show as the scripts and the actors.

Kenny put his glasses back on. Raised his Steinbeck. "Writing sleaze is starting to take its toll on me, man."

I stood up. "How so?"

"Even readin' somebody like Steinbeck. You know, like this really serious, really fine writer. I keep waiting for the sex scenes now."

"Yeah, I can see where that could get to be a problem."

"Like my mom was watchin' *Little Women* the other night on the boob tube."

"Yeah?"

"And all I could think of was how I could turn it into a sleaze book. Like all the sisters are grown up now but they're lesbos."

"Little Lesbos."

"That's exactly the title *I* was thinking of. Exactly, man."

"I'd hold off on that one a while, Kenny."

"Yeah, for one thing, the people who read my books—they probably wouldn't see the parallel to Louisa May Alcott anyway."

Little Lesbos.

At least it was alliterative.

A squat, plump puppy followed me out of the town square and all the way to the sidewalk, then went bounding back to his people.

The heat wasn't too bad yet—still in the low seventies—just the sort of temperature plump little puppies love.

SIX

"I WOULDN'T *EXPECT* YOU to like him, McCain. He's a cultured gentleman."

"Yeah, some cultured gentleman, the way he went after Alger Hiss."

"Alger Hiss is pink right down to his lace panties."

"Nixon himself said that."

"Wrong," she said, pleased, as always, to correct me. "That was Harry Truman himself, McCain."

"Bull roar."

"Bull roar yourself. Look it up. Harry Truman, the darling of the lefties, had a crony out in California he wanted to run for congress. Felt the man could beat Nixon. Then Helen Gahagan Douglas came along and decided to run against Nixon. It was Harry Truman who started the story she was a commie. And Harry Truman who came up with that remark about being pink down to her panties. Dick Nixon merely picked it up."

I would've argued with her but the tale was just unlikely enough to be true. Ever since Ike got in, Democrats have tended to canonize Truman. But you don't want to look too closely or too long at him. Most of us, me certainly included, don't hold up under that kind of scrutiny.

Judge Esme Anne Whitney was fashion-model elegant as ever, poised, prim, and regal against the long windows on the east wall. White summer suit, white pumps, Gauloise cigarette, glass of brandy. We were in her chambers—so much mahogany it was like living in the heart of a tree—and yes it was but eleven a.m. and yes, you did read correctly, a glass of brandy in her slender hand. She claims it helps her concentrate. The amazing thing is that she never shows the merest effect.

I laughed. "Haven't we had this argument before?"

Judge Esme Anne Whitney didn't laugh. Just took another dramatic drag on her Gauloise. "Don't worry, McCain. I won't make you meet him when he comes out here." She shook her head. "You and Ike."

"Me and Ike?"

"The General can't stand him. And poor Dick has always done everything he can to please the man. I like Ike very much, as you know—he and my father used to down shots together in New York after the first war—but I don't think he's ever been very fair about Dick." She turned on me. "And that's why I want you to get this ridiculous snake mess cleared up. My Lord, we'll look like hillbillies. Snakes and Ozark faith healers. Good grief. The man is an intellectual, for God's sake." She frowned. "For once I don't even care about humiliating Cliffie for the sake of my family honor. I just want the culprit caught and put away." She set herself on the edge of her desk. The smoke from her Gauloise was diamond blue in the sunlight.

I lit a Lucky Strike.

"You know how the cops always look around to see who's at a crime scene?"

"Rudimentary police science, McCain."

"Well, I happened to notice two people at the crime scene last night. And you know them both."

"Oh?"

And then she fired the first volley of the morn.

She launched a rubber band slung on her thumb and forefinger. She's good at it. Nine times out of ten she hits me. But she was a little slow this morning. I just angled my head a bit to the left and the rubber band went right on by.

"Who are we talking about here, McCain?"

"We are talking about here, Judge, the good Reverend Thomas C. Courtney and Sara Hall."

"You just don't like Protestants."

"Well, aside from the fact that most of my good friends *are* Protestants, and that I sometimes go to hear Reverend Cosgrove's sermons because he's the most Christ-like man in the whole town, I'd say I do pretty well by you folks. And he's a very conservative Methodist."

"You've never liked Tom. I think you're jealous of him, in fact."

I smiled. "And I probably should be. He seems to have more lady friends than I do." There had been whispers about Courtney and some of his flock. As in fleeced.

"You just couldn't resist saying that, could you?"

I kept on beaming. "No, I couldn't. And I still find it damned strange he'd be out there at the time Muldaur died."

"Meaning what?"

"Meaning nothing other than I find it damned strange. I find Sara Hall being out there even stranger."

"Maybe she went for a ride. She says she does that

sometimes when she feels the urge to take a drink. That was something she learned at her Mayo program. You know, to keep yourself occupied in some way.''

''So she goes for rides with Courtney?''

''What's wrong with that? He's her minister. And it's better than taking a drink, she says.''

She got me with her rubber band this time. Pearl Harbor sneak attack, as I'd been wont to say on the playgrounds of my youth.

''So maybe they were just driving by and saw the ambulance and—''

''I think I'll talk to her.''

''For God's sake, McCain, why?''

''For the same reason I'm going to talk to Courtney. They aren't the type that chase after ambulances. They didn't belong there. Ergo, they're worth talking to.''

''Ergo,'' she said, taking a dramatic drag on her Gauloise.

Her chambers weren't as exciting as they'd once been. In the old days, I came here to see the beautiful Pamela Forrest, to try and get her to go out with me. Nobody could make me feel as bad as Pamela when she turned me down and it was wonderful, anyway. I was drunk on her. And the Judge hated it, was always symbolically hosing me off with harsh words about leaving Pamela alone.

But Pamela was gone. I was still in love with her. It hurt but it wasn't a wonderful hurt anymore. It was a hurt hurt. And for the first time in my life I realized that it was a hurt I'd have to work on getting over. She was out of my life—living elsewhere in shame—and she was never going to be in my life again.

''I want you to promise me you won't go see her.''

''We're talking Sara Hall?''

"We are, as you say, talking Sara Hall."

"She just happened to be out there."

"She just happened to be out there."

"A country-club lady out at a hillbilly church where they use rattlesnakes in their religious ceremonies?"

"Yes."

"And you're not even curious *why* she was out there?"

"No."

"Well," I said, standing up so as to avoid the rubber band she'd just shot at me, "you're the boss."

"Yes, I am, McCain," she smiled with her imperious mouth, "and don't you forget it."

HOW I CAME to talk to Sara Hall twenty minutes later is something I'm not necessarily proud of. I mean, it's the sort of duplicitous thing only a counselor-at-law could come up with. Or a Republican.

Let me put it to you as a philosophical question.

Say there's this woman you want to ask some questions. Now, you've already given your word that you won't go see her.

But what if you happen to be driving by her house and you see her backing out of her driveway in her new DeSoto convertible?

And what if you just happen—not having anything else better to do and the day being so beautiful and all and you owning a red '51 ragtop and it needing to go for a drive to clean some of the engine sludge away and all—you just happen to follow her to our town's first, only, and very tiny—twelve stores—enclosed shopping mall.

And what if you just happen to follow her inside?

And wait while she's in The Moderne Woman? And when she comes out, she runs into you.

You will notice, I believe, the subtle difference between me running into her and her running into me. Which, technically, she did. She could've gone right, she could've gone left, but instead she chose—completely of her own volition—to walk straight.

Now, to be technical again, it is true that I abruptly moved over from my rightward position to be in front of her when she chose—of her own volition—to walk straight ahead. But that's hardly my fault, is it? There was a sudden draft from the nearby air-conditioning duct, and is it my fault I didn't want to catch a head cold and be laid up for weeks? Possibly in traction?

"Hi, Sara."

"Oh, hi, McCain."

Neither time nor alcohol could ever quite dim her beauty. She had a kind of sensibly erotic face, the schoolmarm whose ripe lips told of discreet and memorable pleasures. The brown eyes were sad—you don't drink as much as she did and look happy—but again they were not without aesthetic pleasure, fine brown eyes they were, even with their melancholy, and not without a hint of high intelligent humor even in their gentle pain. White sleeveless blouse, tan tailored skirt, no hose, brown flats. Nice arms.

"That's funny. I just saw the Judge a while ago."

"I talked to her this morning," she said. "She's very excited about Richard Nixon coming out here. It's all she talks about these days." Then, "Nice seeing you."

People ebbed and flowed around us. From the record store came the sound of Jerry Lee Lewis. Teenagers sparked over by the hot-dog counter.

"Say," I said, ever the sly one. "I saw you last night."

"You did?"

"Yes. Out at Muldaur's church."

She actually blushed. "Oh… We were just passing by. And saw the ambulance and everything."

"I thought maybe you knew somebody there. I saw Reverend Courtney."

The flush had faded. An abrupt coldness came into eye and voice. "Yes, we'd taken a ride together. He…helps me sometimes. You know, with—" She hesitated. "You know I went to the Mayo Clinic."

She looked humiliated. Hard to look at pain so fresh in those lovely eyes.

"It's all right, Sara."

"Well, he helps me sometimes. Sort of counsels me."

But if he was the kind and gentle counselor, why had her first reaction been anger when his name came up? And going for a ride together? But then I'd probably been reading too many books by Dr. Edmond DeMille, a/k/a Kenny Thibodeau, and was suspicious of even the most generous acts.

"I really need to go. I'm sorry."

"I didn't mean to bring up anything unpleasant, Sara."

"I know. It's all right."

She touched shapely fingers to the edge of her erotic mouth. "It was nice seeing you."

Wanting to keep her here as long as I could, hoping something useful would just spurt from her, unbidden, I said, "How's your daughter?"

A tiny tic at the outer corner of her left eye. I didn't make much of it. Coincidence.

"Fine. She's just fine." But she sounded tight again, the way she had about Courtney.

"I heard her sing at the springfest in the park. She's got a beautiful voice."

She smiled, looking happy for the first time. "Folk music. The Kingston Trio eighteen hours a day." Then the tic came back. "I need to go. Bye."

I gave her a long minute, then I followed her. There was a bar on the edge of the mall. I hoped I hadn't driven her to it. I felt guilty and confused. Everybody always clucked about her "nervous personality" but her response to what I'd said seemed awfully dramatic. She acted as if I'd accused her of something sinister.

She went into a bookstore. I sat on a bench and smoked a Lucky. I was there two or three minutes when I saw Reverend Courtney appear from the far end of the L-shaped brick mall. He wore a yellow golf shirt and chinos and white Keds. He looked like Yale's most successful graduate of recent vintage. He went into the bookstore, apparently not seeing me, and emerged a bit later in the company of Sara Hall. She looked angry again. Angry but on the verge of cracking, her feelings threatening to overwhelm her.

He had her by the arm, led her to The House of Beef. I'd been there a few times. It was cave-dark, cavern-cold. It was the preferred trysting place. The martinis were good, the food better. All the upwardly mobile young men who imagined themselves to be cool—a la Peter Gunn or Tony Curtis I suppose— called the place "The House," the way Frank Sinatra would.

I wondered if she'd drink. I wondered if she'd cry.

I wondered if she'd get violent. She'd seemed on the verge of all three. And then I wondered if she was in love with Courtney. It was the kind of thought I didn't especially want to have. I'd always liked Sara Hall.

SEVEN

I SPENT HALF AN hour at the gas station where I get my ragtop worked on. Being a Saturday, they were busy with cars up on the hoist. I'd stopped in just to schedule a time for a tune-up but I liked the particular atmosphere of the place—the smell of gasoline and oil, the clank of tools hitting the concrete, the hoist that lifts and lowers the cars—and the male camaraderie that is second only to a barbershop. Taverns don't count for camaraderie because alcohol skews everything. But barbershops and gas stations…that's where men are men. And someday I plan to be one of them.

The topics today included how bad the Cubs were doing, how much/how little they looked forward to Nixon visiting our town, the high-school girls parading up and down the sidewalk in short-shorts (''God, I wish they woulda worn 'em that short back when *I* was in school!''), how Jack Kennedy's wife walked like she had a cob up her ass (Republicans) or looked like a glamorous movie star (Democrats), and finally how Muldaur's murder was inevitable, him being the center of ''all them nuts out to his church.''

The gas-station consensus was that one of Muldaur's own had done him in. Nobody mentioned Muldaur's affinity for cheating on his wife. In fact, they didn't offer any specific reason for his being killed. They just felt that anybody who messed around with snakes the way he did was bound to come to no good.

I stopped by Rexall for lunch, bought a new John D. MacDonald paperback and a copy of *Galaxy*, which I read through while I ate my burger and fries. While I was sitting at the counter, I saw Muldaur's sergeant-at-arms towering above the patent medicines in aisle three. He wore a worn, blue work shirt and was the strapping size of Muldaur himself, but there was nothing messianic about his face. He looked well-attached to reality, and not all that happy about whatever his particular reality was doing to him. I left a tip and slid down off the stool.

I started toward him but decided this wouldn't be a good place to talk. There was a lull in business. Too easy for people to overhear. The quiet would intimidate him.

I followed him outdoors after he bought a carton of Wings and a bottle of Pepto-Bismol. He made his way toward a pickup truck that had once been a Model-T. The back half had been sawed off and two-by-fours set in behind the front seats. It was the kind of truck that got a lot of poor families through the Depression.

After he'd climbed in and started the engine, which sounded pretty damned smooth given the age of the vehicle, I went up to him and said, "I'm afraid I don't know your name."

"So what?"

"You remember me from the other night?"

"Yeah. You were with that Jew girl."

"What makes you think she was Jewish?"

"They smell."

"Why don't you keep your filthy mouth shut?"

"You just can't take the truth."

"What truth?"

"That bringing a Jew in there is what killed him."

"So it was her fault, huh?"

He patted a Bible on the seat next to him. It had an outsize golden cross on its imitation leather cover. And next to the Bible was a stack of his leaflets about Jews and Catholics. "Jews killed Our Lord. They start trouble wherever they go."

I wanted to laugh. I'd had the same problem with Hitler. He was, for all his evil, laughable. His theories of a "pure race" were ridiculous on their face. Thousands and thousands of years ago, the Vikings visited most places on the planet. And they were one randy bunch of guys, let me tell you. There hadn't been a "pure" race since. In fact, it's doubtful even the Vikings were a pure race. That's the trouble with evil sometimes—it turns into farce.

Jews smell. The presence of a Jew had caused a murder to take place. Uh-huh.

"I'm curious about something."

He ground the car into gear. Sounded as if the transmission teeth needed a little work. I notice stuff like that.

"I don't want to talk to you anymore."

"I saw you slap a woman the other night. Was that your wife?"

He grabbed me. So quickly, so skillfully that I wasn't sure what happened till it was over. He flung me back across the sidewalk, propelling me into a corner mailbox.

He pulled away.

I shouted, trying to recover at least a modicum of dignity for the interested bystanders, "Was Muldaur

sleeping with your wife? Was that why you slappe-
dher?"

A guy the town seemed to employ as a wise guy—
he'd always been here, I'd never seen him gainfully
employed, he just kinda wandered around and made
sarcastic remarks, a modern version of the Greek cho-
rus—said, "Good thing he took off. Otherwise you
would've killed him, McCain."

The groundlings who were standing around all
looked at me and laughed.

I WASTED AN hour walking around to the various print
shops. Half of them were closed on such a baking Saturday afternoon and the other half claimed that they
didn't know anything about who'd printed the leaflets
and the slick pamphlets that came from Muldaur's
church and were plastered all over town. Most people
of all denominations found them disgusting and com-
plained about them in *The Clarion* letters column.

In a small town like ours, you have to be very careful of who you offend. There were just enough Catholics that printing Muldaur's hate mail could cost you
any Catholic business you had.

But if anyone knew anything, they weren't talking
about it. Only one person gave me anything remotely
resembling a lead. He said that there was a former
press operator who now had a small press in his basement and did odd jobs. He'd taken a full-time job in
the Amana factory where they made freezers because
the pay was so much better. The guy said he didn't
know if Parnell, the former press operator, had done
the Muldaur work but that he was probably worth
checking out. He gave me Parnell's address. I thanked

him. I'd gone to Catholic school with Parnell. We hadn't been friends, but then we hadn't been enemies.

REVEREND COURTNEY was sitting on his church steps talking to a dowager in a summer frock and a large summer hat. They looked quite handsome, the church of native stone magnificent in the afternoon light, the large front lawn well-tended and very green, a water-color cover from *The New Yorker* perhaps, even a breeze cooperating by fluttering the long blue ribbon that trailed from the dowager's hat.

Her name was Helen Prentice, and she and her husband were not only wealthy but also generous. There wasn't a hospital, library, or auditorium within a hundred miles in any direction that the Prentices hadn't contributed substantially to.

"Hello, Sam," Helen said, extending her hand. We shook. I'd met her at various soirees at Judge Whitney's house.

"Afternoon, Helen."

She checked her watch. "I need to run."

Courtney, now in dark slacks and a white shirt, started to raise himself from the church step but she stopped him with a gloved white hand.

"The last time I checked, Reverend, I wasn't royalty. There's no need to stand." She smiled at me. "George and I really enjoyed sitting with you at the Judge's dinner table last month. You're a very funny young man." Then back to Courtney. "See you in the morning at the ten o'clock service."

When she was out of earshot, or so he assumed, he said, "There goes one very rich lady, McCain."

"I'd think that a man who'd dedicated himself to following in the footsteps of Jesus might also point out

that she's a very decent person, too. Very generous
with her riches.''

"Nice to know you're not afraid of being pompous.''

I said, "How was the food at The House today?''

He wasn't intimidated. "I knew you were an unsuccessful lawyer. I guess I'd forgotten that you were an
unsuccessful gumshoe, too.''

"You and Sara Hall just happened to be driving
around last night and ended up at Muldaur's church
completely by coincidence?''

"That's right, McCain.''

He looked vital and modern standing against the
massive medieval-style doors of the church. "I'm sorry
I got you Catholics in a tizzy by quoting Dr. Peale. It's
a free country, you know. Or so they tell me, anyway.''

"Right now, I'm more interested in you and Sara
Hall. What were you *really* doing out there last night?''

He smiled. He had great teeth, of course. Movie-star
teeth. "As I said, I'm told it's a free country. Or didn't
they teach you that in that second-rate law school you
went to?''

He came down off the steps and walked over to
where a rake leaned against an elm. From his back
pocket he took a pair of brown work gloves, cinched
them on, and started raking.

As I WALKED back to my office, I noticed leaflets on
car windows, placed under windshield wipers. A block
before I reached my place I saw a boy of maybe twelve
toting an armload of the leaflets and getting punched
in the face by a much bigger kid. The Flannagan boy.
Flannagan was no doubt displeased with the anti-
Catholic nature of the leaflets. But mostly he just liked

punching kids smaller than him. Flannagan, who'd played fullback on the Catholic school varsity squad until they realized he didn't have any talent, was born to bully.

I got between them and gave Flannagan a shove.

"What're you stoppin' me for, McCain? You see that shit he's got about Catholics? He says we ain't Americans."

"You're a lot bigger than he is, Flannagan."

"I don't care. He still deserves to be punched."

Nice to know that Muldaur's work was living on beyond him. He'd brought the town to a boil in life—and the water was still hot now that he'd died.

"Who told you to pass these out?" I said to the kid. He wore bib overalls with a striped T-shirt. He had freckles and a cowlick and a squirt of blood in his right nostril from Flannagan's fist. And bare feet. I was surprised he wasn't dancing a jig.

"God told me to," he said.

I almost laughed.

"God," Flannagan said. "My ass."

"You shouldn't talk like that. Dirty, I mean," the kid said. "My mom says Catholics and Jews talk like that all the time."

Now I'll double back on what I said earlier about the foolish side of evil. There's nothing more frightening than a youngster who has been completely indoctrinated by his parents. He's as soulless as a robot and as deadly as an assassin. You can't reason with him because the "on" switch in his brain doesn't operate. His parents turned it off permanently long ago.

"Why don't you let me take those?" I said.

I reached for the leaflets and he jumped back a foot.

"No! You're a dirty Catholic just like Flannagan here."

"You call me a dirty Catholic again and I'll knock you out."

"Shut up, Flannagan," I said. "Kid, I want the leaflets."

"They're mine and you can't take them away from me."

"Let me handle him, McCain," Flannagan said, "c'mon."

And with that, not unexpectedly, the kid took off running down the sidewalk. Flannagan lunged, as if he were going after him. I grabbed him by the shoulder.

"I should be able to hit him if I want to," he said.

"Yes," I said, "that's one of your inalienable rights. Punching kids who weigh forty pounds less than you do."

"He hates Catholics."

"Or at least his parents do."

"Huh?"

"Never mind."

His moon face tightened into a sneer. "You mind if I go now, your royal highness?"

"Always a pleasure to see you, Flannagan." There are some people you just don't want on your side.

As I climbed into my ragtop and headed home, I tried not to think about some of the feelings that Jack Kennedy seemed to stir up. Otherwise reasonable, decent people still had their bias toward Catholics in office. William Jennings Bryan always said that he wished he hadn't run for president because it taught him just how deep anti-Catholic and anti-Jewish bias ran in this country. Things had improved since then but, as with Dr. Norman Vincent Peale, even respectable ministers felt safe in talking about Kennedy as a stalking horse for the pope.

Then there were the unrespectable people—the Klan, the Nazi sympathizers left over from the German American Bund days of the big war, the small-town radio ministers, the pamphleteers of every description. There'd been an article in *Time* magazine a few years back noting that any fund-raising letter or pamphlet with the word "Jew," "Communist," "Catholic," or "Negro" in its headline would earn twice as much money as a letter or pamphlet without. Judging by the entertainment shows on the tube, everything was just okey-dokey here in the land of Lincoln. But we knew better, didn't we?

EIGHT

I PARKED IN BACK OF my apartment house, meaning to wash my car the way I usually did on late Saturday afternoons. Mrs. Goldman had a nice two-stall garage with a hose.

I was about halfway to the house when I heard the music. It wasn't all that loud but it was an odd choice for Mrs. Goldman. Miles Davis. I wondered when she'd gotten interested in jazz. She liked Broadway tunes and singers like Patti Page and Kay Starr.

I had just reached the stairs that run up the back and lead to my apartment when I realized that the music was coming from my place, not Mrs. Goldman's.

The windows were open and so, partially, was the back door. I went inside.

She sat in the big leather armchair. She wore a white blouse that displayed her lovely breasts discreetly, a pair of dark blue shorts that did equally nice things for her long legs, and a pair of white tennis shoes. She had a tanned, tight body and that impish damned face that could go sentimental on you all of a sudden and make you sad. I'd never had a crush on a married woman before and I didn't want to now. But here she was in my apartment. There was a half-full bottle of J&B scotch and a Peter Pan peanut-butter glass sitting on the arm of the chair.

"You bastard," she said from the couch, where she was reclining.

"Nice to see you too, Kylie."

"You're late," she said, all hot accusation.

"Late for what?"

"For our job interview." She was slurring her words but I'll spare you the drunk dialect.

"Kylie, did you by any chance drink half of that bottle of scotch?"

"What half bottle of scotch?"

"The one next to your hand."

"My hand?"

She was in fine shape. A drinker she was not. I'd seen her get snockered once on two beers. The toll the scotch took had to be devastating.

"So where were you?"

"Working, actually," I said.

"Working actually? Who's actually?" Then she grinned, looking pretty damned cute. "I told a funny."

"Yes, you did."

"You're late."

"You said that. But I didn't realize we had an appointment."

She shook her head. She was so loaded she had to squint one eye to see me. There were probably multiple me's, the way I'd be perceived by a fly. "Job interview."

"What job interview are we talking about?"

"*We* aren't talking about a job interview. *I* am talking about a job interview."

"All right." I went over and sat down on the couch and got a Lucky going. "And what job interview would that be?"

"I want to hire you to kill my husband."

"Well, that sounds reasonable enough. What's the pay?"

"I could give you a hundred down. And a hundred more later on. When I get my paycheck."

"Well, I do have a gun, I guess."

She squinted again. Her head was rotating as if on a track of ball bearings. "You got any bullets?"

"A few."

"How many's a few?"

"Probably a couple dozen."

"Good, 'cause I want you to shoot him at least that many times." Then, "Where's that damned bottle?"

"I think it got on a bus and went to Cleveland in self-defense."

She either didn't hear—or didn't care to hear—my joke.

"There it is."

Watching her pour a drink was like watching a high-wire act. There was a lot of danger. It did things to your bowels and heart and the palms of your hands. Somehow she managed to get it poured without (a) cracking the glass when the neck of the bottle slammed against the rim, (b) spilling any on the chair, or (c) spilling any on herself.

"Then I want you to set him on fire."

"Shoot him first. Then set him on fire. Got it."

"He's a jerk. I just can't believe how *much* of a jerk."

"You know, Miles Davis may not be the best music for you to be listening to right now," I said.

"I need to be sad."

"Well, ole Miles'll help you get there."

"Who you want to hear? Frankie Avalon?"

"Why don't I just turn it off?"

I got up and turned it off and then went over to the refrigerator. "You had anything to eat lately?"

"Last night."

"You haven't eaten since last night?"

"Too mad to eat." And again her head rolled free on the ball bearings. "That jerk." Then she belched. It was a cute little belch. "Excuse me."

"How about a bologna sandwich?"

"Didn't I just say excuse me?"

"Yes, you did. And you are excused. Now how about I fix you a bologna sandwich?"

"With ketchup?"

"If you want some."

"I'm not all that hungry."

"You need some food. Believe me."

"The first place you should shoot him is right in the crotch."

"Poetic justice, eh?"

"D. nn right."

I made her a bologna sandwich.

She said, as I was making it, her head rolling around more violently than ever, "What happened to Ray Charles?"

"You weren't listening to Ray Charles. You were listening to Miles Davis." We liked a lot of the same jazz records.

"I was not. I was listening to Ray Charles. 'Green Dolphin Street.'"

"You were listening to Miles Davis, and 'Green Dolphin Street' is Tony Bennett, anyway."

I served her a sandwich on a saucer. "Sit up."

"Why?"

"So you can digest this better."

"What happened to Dakota Staton?" Dakota being a jazz singer we both liked very much.

I decided not to go back through it. "I turned off the music."

She stared—through a fly's eye again, no doubt—at her sandwich, looking as if nobody'd ever before put such a thing in front of her. "Did I tell you you should shoot him in the crotch?"

"Duly noted."

"What's that mean?"

"It means, yes, you told me, and yes, I'll remember it."

"What's this?"

"A bologna sandwich."

"I'm not hungry."

"You need to eat. Now, c'mon."

Her head wobbled and she glanced up at me. "How come you're so short?"

"How come you're so drunk?"

"Shoot him in the crotch *twice*."

"Eat."

"We should get some grenades, is what we should get."

She ate.

Two bites. Then, "You know what I found in his billfold?"

"What?"

"Picture of her."

"I'm sorry."

"He carries a picture of her around with him."

"C'mon, just eat."

"Just like she's his wife or something."

"Eat."

She ate, all right. About six, seven bites altogether.

Then it—and a lot of the scotch—came right back up. Luckily I got her to the john in time.

There was a fan going in the bedroom window. I positioned her as comfortably as possible on the bed and then let my three cats Tasha, Crystal, and Tess— well, technically, a friend of mine named Samantha left them with me when she went to Hollywood hoping to find gold and glamour—situate themselves around her.

The next four hours were pretty boring so let's just say that I watched some TV, I fixed myself a couple of burgers, I fed the cats, and I looked in on Kylie every once in a while. I felt bad for her. Having chased the beautiful Pamela Forrest all those years, I knew all about heartbreak. Or at least I fancied I did. Me and Robert Ryan. But actually never having been married...wow, your mate comes home and admits that he's seeing somebody else—which is what I guessed had happened—that was head-in-the-oven time.

The heat broke around nine. Kylie got up and went in the john. She wasn't in there very long. I got a glimpse of her when she came out. She was walking that stiff-armed way Boris Karloff always does when he plays Frankenstein's monster. She went right back to bed.

I barely heard the knock. The fan was kicking out and the TV was on. I wouldn't have noticed the door at all if Tess hadn't trotted over there. She's kind of a watch cat. She can't bark but if you come in and she's got her doubts about you, she bites you on the ankle.

He let himself in. And Tess bit him on the ankle.

"Hey!" he said.

He was tall and blond and handsome, I suppose, but in a preppy way I've always resented. Or been jealous of. Take your pick.

The one and only Chad Burke.

'What's with your cat? She bit me.''

"She's discriminating."

He said, "She here?"

"Yeah."

He looked around. "Where?"

"Bedroom."

I'd gotten up and walked over to him. He started toward me now. Angry. "You didn't screw her, did you?"

"No," I said. "And I guess you didn't, either. Your new girlfriend wouldn't like that, would she?"

The anger vanished as quickly as it had appeared. He ran a long, artistic hand through his curly blond hair. He looked miserable. "All I asked her for was a little time. I didn't say I'd leave her. I just said I needed to work through it. She made a big deal of it."

"Gee, how insensitive of her."

"I told her when I married her, writers are pretty messed-up people. Being creative isn't easy. You know, like actors."

I decided not to tell him that (a) he wasn't a writer but a grad school dabbler, (b) that even if he was a real writer it didn't give him any license to cheat on his wife, and (c) everybody knew that most actors were morons anyway.

He said, "You really didn't screw her?"

"I really didn't screw her."

"That's what I figured she'd do. You know, go out and sleep with you. She likes you."

"She did want to hire me to kill you. But that was for money. She didn't mention anything about sex."

He didn't smile.

"That'd just make things worse," he said, "she goes out and starts grudge-screwing people."

"But it's all right if you nail your student?"

"That's different. That doesn't have anything to do with spite. I'm half in love with her."

"Ah. Now I get the distinction."

He glared at me. "I'm not asking for your approval, McCain. I could give a shit what you think about me. Now, I've got my car out back and I'm going to go in there and get her and take her home. And you're not going to stop me."

"She's your wife, Chad. But let me tell you something."

He waved me off. "Believe me, I've heard it all already. All day long I've heard it. She called her folks and they called my folks. All I've done all day is argue with people. And try and justify myself. What can I say? Diane is good for my writing. I'm just more creative when she's in my life." And then he got a little more intimate. Male-to-male. "And she's not the prude Kylie is. I mean, this is a terrible thing to say but Kylie isn't so hot in the sack."

I hit him. Right in the mouth. And he hit me. Right in the mouth. I wasn't tough but then neither was he. What he was was tall. So I kept pounding him in the stomach and in the ribs. And he kept pounding me on the top and the sides of the head. The cats all scattered, howling. We knocked a floor lamp over, then a table lamp.

And that's when Kylie came out, sweet in her mussed hair and wrinkled clothes, her little-girl fist grinding sleep out of her eyes. "Is this a dream?"

"It sure isn't a dream," Chad said. "Some friends you've got. He hit me."

She surveyed the living and kitchen areas. "God, you guys broke stuff. That's what woke me up." Then, "You okay, McCain?"

"Yeah, I'm fine."

"I see." Chad pouted. "You ask about him but you don't ask about me. I just happen to be your husband."

And a writer, too, Chad. Don't forget you're a deeply tormented writer.

This time when Tess went to the door, it was the inside one. I expected I knew who it was. I opened it and there she stood, the best-looking landlady in the universe. Tall, graceful, gray subtly streaking her long, dark hair, mid-fifties. Mrs. Goldman. One beautiful babe. "Are you all right, Sam? I heard all this commotion and—" She looked behind me to where Kylie and Chad stood. "Oh, hello. I'm Kate Goldman."

Chad said, "He attacked me."

Mrs. Goldman smiled. "You're an awful lot bigger than he is."

"And for what it's worth, McCain," Chad said, "I'm not so sure I believe you about you and Kylie." Then, to Kylie: "Will you get your damned shoes on so we can get out of here?" Then, to me: "And if I find out you *weren't* telling me the truth, McCain, you're going to be damned sorry, believe me."

Kylie went on her groggy, uncertain way. Got her tennis shoes on untied and came back to the living room. "I'm sorry, McCain." Then she gave me a peck on the cheek.

"You kiss him right in front of me?" Chad said. He looked at Mrs. Goldman. "Did you see that? Right in front of her own husband, she kisses him!"

"Yes," Mrs. Goldman said. "I was shocked."

He frowned. He had quite a frown. "I should've known you'd be just like him."

"Chad's folks bought him a new car," Kylie said brightly. "Maybe I'll get lucky and puke all over it."

As they left, Tess bit him on the ankle again. He tried to kick her but she was too quick for him.

The air was unsettled, like a battleground in the aftermath.

"Gosh, I sure hope to see a lot more of him, McCain."

"You no doubt will. He's going to be famous."

"Oh?"

"He's a writer. Just ask him."

"That poor girl. I see her at temple every once in a while in Iowa City. But I've never really gotten to know her. How could she have married a jerk like that?"

Kate Goldman's husband, who was by all accounts a very nice guy, died several years ago. Mrs. Goldman now dated men from the synagogue in Iowa City. I was personally pulling for this history teacher at City High. One night on the porch downstairs he'd told me about his time in Italy during the war and then we ended up talking about paperback writers. His two favorites were David Goodis and Day Keene. I was hoping he'd run for president some day.

"Gosh," Mrs. Goldman said, "I really like your new friend here, Sam." She fanned herself with a slender hand. She wore a crisp pink blouse and black walking shorts and black flats. If Lauren Bacall had any luck, she'd end up looking just like Kate Goldman when she got older. "This place is a mess."

"Yeah, I'm sorry."

"I'm sure it wasn't your fault."

I got the broom and dustpan and we got busy.

Afterward, I poured us each a beer and we sat around and talked about Dick Nixon coming to town and how Jack Kennedy was holding up, and then we talked local news, her wanting to know all about my visit to Muldaur's church. "Boy, I sure wouldn't handle any of those snakes."

A summer storm started right after Mrs. Goldman left, August heat lightning stalking the sky like huge electric spiders. It got hotter and even more humid for a time and then it got much cooler suddenly. I lay on my bed with a beer and a cigarette reading a collection of Irwin Shaw short stories. The rain came around ten o'clock, a Biblical rain. In the valley where the city park was the sewers would flood and some of the park benches and picnic tables would float a few yards away, and at the next city council meeting somebody would stand up and suggest that we chain the benches and the tables to nearby trees so this catastrophe would never be visited upon us again.

Whenever the call came—in that state that is neither sleep nor waking—I was standing at the altar and a guy in a funny religious hat and a lot of funny religious capes and vestments was reading from one of Kenny Thibodeau's racy novels—I think the title was *Lesbo Lawyers*—and saying, "I now pronounce you husband and wives." And there I stood with the beautiful Pamela Forrest and the fetching Mary Travers and—

"Hullo."

"McCain?"

"I think so."

"Very funny."

"What time is it?"

"Four thirty-seven. You should be up."

"Uh-huh."

"Do you have any idea why I'm calling?"

"Do I win a prize if I guess right?"

"I'm calling because I figured that you hadn't heard the news yet."

"What news?"

And then she told me and I abruptly came awake.

"I want you to get over there before Cliffie mucks everything up."

"I'm on my way, Judge."

"When you get done over there, call me."

"How'd you find out about it?"

"I keep a police radio on very low next to my bed. If anything important happens, the dispatcher begins to screech. That wakes me up."

There was something very lonely about that but then the lady'd had four—or was it five?—husbands so I guessed she was lonely by choice.

I jerked on some clothes and ran downstairs to my ragtop.

PART II

NINE

THE WAY I GOT all this—mostly from an auxiliary cop named Coggins who had a thermos full of wonderful-smelling coffee—was that around midnight Iris Courtney started worrying about her husband. She told Cliffie (Coggins apparently being present) that shortly after that time she got a strange call from her husband. He said that she was not to worry but that he was involved in something and would explain when he got home. She said he'd sounded anxious but not afraid. At three a.m., frightened now, she walked out to the garage to see if something might have happened to him. She recalled hearing a story on the radio about a man who pulled his car into the garage, had a heart attack, slumped over on the seat, and was not discovered until morning when it was too late. She didn't want this to happen to her husband. She went out and checked the garage. She saw that his car was there and immediately began to panic. She began to frantically search the alley. And that's when she looked between her garage and the one belonging to their neighbors. He was lying on his back, staring up at the quarter-moon that looked so fresh after the rain. She saw that he'd been stabbed many times in the chest. His yellow shirt was soaked dark with blood. A neighbor's dog was crouched nearby—a rather stupid-looking beagle, she noted—staring at the corpse as if it could not understand what was going on here. Usually, the minister was so friendly and playful with the dog. She immediately went in and called the police station.

She was inside the rectory with Cliffie now.

Dawn was still an hour away but neighbors were beginning to drift into the alley where Doc Novotony was looking over the corpse. Everybody looked well turned-out given the time of day. Most of them had put on street clothes. Few wore robes.

Coggins kept them away from the strip of grass between the garages by waving the beam of his red-capped flashlight to the right. "Nothing to see, folks. Don't get in the doc's way now."

Dick Coggins was the best of the auxiliary cops. In fact, he was smarter than any of the cops on the regular force. But because he wasn't a member of the Sykes clan, and despite scoring high on all the state tests for peace officers, he was kept on reserve status. In the meantime, he drove a panel truck for an office-supply company and played a lot of softball. He could throw a softball about as fast as anybody I'd ever seen. He was tall, trim, wore his dark hair in a crew-cut and spoke with a faint Virginia drawl. He'd spent his first eleven years there.

"I should've figured you'd be here, Sam," he said. "I could've brought your book back."

He borrowed my textbooks on criminology and police procedure. He knew all about crime scenes and how to set them up.

"You able to beat Cliffie to the punch tonight?"

He smiled. "Well, I got here before he trampled all over everything. I'll give all the evidence to Theresa at the hospital, same as I did with Muldaur's stuff."

Theresa was a lab tech and a girl he dated. Since Cliffie hated to send anything to the state lab—feeling apparently that it robbed him of his authority as el comandante—Theresa was the best we could do locally.

"I'll call her."

"Sure."

The press was here now. A rumpled, sleepy reporter with a microphone and a heavy tape recorder slung over his shoulder wandered from one neighbor to the other asking all the usual obvious, stupid questions. I'm waiting for the wife of a recently murdered man to say to a reporter, "How does it feel to have your husband murdered? I'll tell you, It feels great. He was an arrogant, overbearing jerk and I want to thank whoever killed him. I can finally live like a normal human being now that old Ralph is gone." Just once.

The crowd grew. The ambulance team took the body away. Doc Novotony yawned a lot. Cliffie gave the radio guy one of his Dick Tracy Crime Fighter speeches—this case was going to be wrapped up within forty-eight hours and you had his word on it—and then said (honest), "Some people thought that Reverend Courtney was sort of a snob and thought *he* was better than the rest of us because he was from back east, but I felt that deep down he was just a regular guy. Let's not forget that he was a Cubs fan."

Maybe they'd let him give the graveside remarks.

I HAD TO appear before Judge Ronald D.K.M. Sullivan that morning. Don't ask what the initials stand for. Local lawyers insist that they translate to Duly Krazy Mick. And that would certainly apply. D.K.M. has two modes—confused and very, very, which is to say extremely, pissed off. He has been known to hum, whittle an apple and eat it, do deep breathing exercises, and flip coins while you're making your case before his bench. He berates you for the color, cut, and cleanliness of your suit. He reminds you when you need a haircut. He has advised young women to wear more uplifting bras and young men to wear toupees because the sunlight streaming through his courtroom windows is brilliant when bounced off a bald pate. His nose runs, his eyes collect pounds of green stuff in the corners, and the last time he brushed his teeth we were bombing Berlin. He is, as near as anyone can guess, somewhere between two hundred and four hundred years old. Like those turtles.

He said, "And what offense against humanity has Mr. Larkin committed today, Mr. McCain?"

"He's been charged with obstructing justice."

"Obstructing justice?" He made it sound as if he'd never heard the words before.

"He is alleged to have struck an officer who was trying to arrest Mr. Larkin's lady friend."

"And why was the officer trying to arrest Mr. Larkin's lady friend?"

"Because allegedly his lady friend had kicked the officer in the crotch area."

"And for what reason had his lady friend kicked the officer in the crotchtal area?"

The crotchtal area? Crotchtal? D.K.M always tried to make things sound a little more dignified than they are. Hence, crotchtal area. And by the way, all the things he makes me explain? Most judges read the charges before they have you address the bench. But D.K.M. saves time by having *you* do all his prep for him.

"She kicked him in the crotchtal area because he called her a name."

"And what name would that be, Mr. McCain?"

"He called her a hooker."

"A what?"

"A hooker. It's slang for prostitute."

"Ah, a strumpet."

"Something like that."

"So the officer of the law calls the lady friend of Mr. Larkin a strumpet and she kicks him in the crotchtal area and when the officer of the law tries to arrest her Mr. Larkin steps in and strikes the officer of the law in the face?"

"That's correct, Your Honor."

"Good. Now I understand. And by the way, Mr. McCain, you really need a haircut."

I wanted to kick him in the crotchtal area.

I DIDN'T GET in to see Judge Whitney until much later that morning. And when I did get to her chambers, I found two men and two women I'd never seen before. They had the taint of fussiness about them, a certain archness that stamped them as her kind of folk, not mine. One of the women was a nice-looking redhead. Which reminded me of Kylie Burke. I wondered how she was doing. Her world had to be coming apart. No matter that she was too good for him. She'd always been so clearly gaga over him that it was painful to watch.

The Judge was giving orders like a field commander. "Then, Rick, you know how I want the tent set up. And Randy you know how I wanted the cake to be made—eight tiers. And Darla I want the food to be as colorfully arranged as Michele's flowers—in fact, you two should get together and see if there's some way you could coordinate some things.''

Maybe a gardenia sandwich, I thought.

All this was for Richard Milhous Nixon, of course.

I had seen the Judge a-flutter and a-twitter before but these had been on separate occasions. But I'd never seen her both a-flutter and a-twitter at the same time. This was something to behold.

Oleg Cassini had become her designer of choice and so on her four-trips-a-year to New York City she stocked up on Cassini duds the way factory workers stocked up on Monkey Wards work clothes. Today, she wore a handsome tan linen suit with matching pumps. Her short hair looked freshly washed and combed. And she strode the length of her office with runway elegance. She was all crazed, nervous energy, terrified that she'd make less than a good impression on old Milhous.

That's why you have to be careful about being a-flutter and a-twitter at the same time. It can really make you crazy—you're like an engine with the idle running too fast.

''Now, does everybody know what they need to do?''

Cowed, terrified, they glanced at each other and then looked back at the Judge. They nodded like frightened puppies who'd just pooped on the new carpeting.

''Good, because I don't need to tell you, there'll be hell to pay for anybody who screws up.''

I felt sorry for them. God, I felt sorry for them.

She waved them dismissively away. They left with great hurried relief.

''So,'' she said when the last of them had closed the door, ''this thing is getting worse and worse.''

She went over to her desk, poured herself some brandy, plucked a Gauloise from her cigarette case and lighted it with a small aluminum box that somehow produced fire.

"They're connected," she said, exhaling a gulf stream of blue smoke. "Muldaur and Reverend Courtney."

"I sure think so."

"But how?"

"Not a clue. Not so far."

"I don't want these ridiculous murders hanging over our heads when Dick gets here." A chic sip. She was a damned good-looking woman and knew it. "You have one of your famous lists?"

"I have one of my famous lists."

My crime instructor at the university said that a good detective always writes down names and incidents and then begins to connect them, like children's puzzles where eventually the connected lines draw a picture. In this case, the picture of a killer.

"The night Muldaur was murdered, both Sara Hall and the now-deceased Reverend Courtney just happened to show up. I find that strange. I mean, why would they be way out in the boonies like that? That's the first thing on my list. The second thing is that when I went out to Muldaur's trailer the day after the murder the daughter said she knew who'd killed her father but then her mother told her to shut up. Also, there was a crazy hillbilly there named Ned. He was exchanging bullets with the Muldaurs, which they explained to me was just a mountain tradition and not anything to worry about. He claims that Muldaur owes him money for collecting snakes. He's worth following up on and so is the daughter, Ella. Item three on my list is Sara Hall again. I know you told me not to bother her but I just happened to run into her out at the shopping mall.''

''I'll bet you just happened to run into her.''

''She looked very rocky. Scared, angry, confused. Take your pick. Or maybe all three. Anyway, after she left me she met the good Reverend Courtney. They went into The House of Beef together.''

''I wonder what that was all about.''

''So do I.''

Her face twisted with displeasure. ''She wasn't having an affair with him, was she?''

''She's your friend, Judge. You'd know better than I would.''

She walked over to the long, leaded window that overlooked the courthouse lawn. She loved to pose dramatically in front of it. Maybe she was practicing for Milhous.

''Did she ever mention Courtney to you?'' I said. ''Did she say why he was counseling Dierdre?''

''Not really. But Dierdre's always had problems. Depression. She saw her father drown.''

The story was well-known locally. Extremely wealthy man trying out his brand-new Chris-Craft one late Fourth of July on the river when a speedboat being driven by a monumentally drunken local playboy smashed into him. The wealthy man—Art Hall—drowned after rescuing his wife and daughter. Dierdre went back in the water after her father. Bystanders had to restrain her from doing it again. She spent a fair amount of time in a mental hospital shortly after that. She was thirteen years old at the time, probably seventeen now. The playboy had some good lawyers. He quickly moved to California and had not been heard from since.

You saw Dierdre walking around town. One of her doctors had apparently told her that exercise was good for combating depression. So she walked. Everywhere. Day and night. She had yet to finish high school. She hadn't attended the previous semester. Depression. She had a prim, Victorian beauty except for the troubled eyes. She favored heavy sweaters, jeans, white Keds. Even in the summer, when other people wore the least the law would allow, there would be Dierdre in her cable-knit sweater. Walking.

"You want to talk to Sara?"

She shook her head. "I'll have you do it. I value her friendship too much. She'll resent it coming from me."

"She'll resent it coming from me, too."

She smiled. "Yes, but I don't really give a damn about that, do I? Now get out there and find out what's going on, McCain. When my people ran this town, we didn't have any unsolved murders, believe me."

The thing was, for all the puffery, the statement was probably true. If nothing else, the Whitneys are bright and tidy and efficient civil servants.

At the door, she said, "Muldaur being killed did one good thing, anyway."

"What?"

"No more of those damned anti-Semitic and anti-Catholic flyers he was putting out. And I say that as a Protestant, McCain. You know I don't have a prejudiced bone in my body. I'm very happy that all you people came over here on your little boats."

I could tell she wanted some sort of Nobel peace prize for saying what she'd just said. Unfortunately, I didn't have one on me to give her.

TEN

I HEARD GIRLISH GIGGLING as I walked through my office door. Kylie was parked with great poise upon the edge of my desk and Jamie was sitting behind her typewriter stand. They both were smoking filtered cigarettes and drinking Pepsi from bottles.

"God," Kylie was saying, "so how did you get your clothes back?"

"That's the thing," Jamie was saying. "We didn't. The dog dragged them off. We never found them again."

"Then how'd you get home?"

"We drove back on dirt roads and then we had to take alleys all the way to my house. I had to get a blanket from the garage and sneak into the house. I was afraid my dad was gonna wake up and see me in my birthday suit."

Giggling again. They were as drunk as they could get on Pepsi. There was something sweet about it. Kylie was a city girl with a brain and Jamie was a small-town girl with a body. And yet here they were fast friends, at least for this small inconsequential moment in this backwoods town in this backwoods state on this backwoods planet in the vast, indifference universe. Every once in a while, I try to put things into perspective. It was those damned philosophy courses I took.

I went behind my desk and sat down. Kylie, cautiously erotic in a prim white blouse and tight royal blue skirt, pushed her Pepsi at me and said, "Jamie's been telling me about the night she and Turk went skinny-dipping."

"Good old Turk," I said.

"Mr. C's never met Turk," Jamie said.

"And I'm the poorer for it, no doubt," I said.

"Turk sounds sort of cool, actually," Kylie said, relishing the effect her words would have on me.

"Oh, yes, very cool," I said.

"As opposed to short, mouthy guys who *aren't* cool."

Jamie giggled. "I think she's talking about you, Mr. C."

At which point a horn sounded.

"Turk!" Jamie said. "He's picking me up for lunch!"

"I hope he's got clothes on," Kylie laughed.

"She'd make you a great girlfriend," Jamie said of Kylie. "I mean, if you weren't all hung up on that snob Pam Forrest. And if Kylie wasn't married."

"You have a succinct way of stating a problem," Kylie said.

"I don't know what succinct means but it sounds sort of dirty."

The horn again.

"He'll have to come in sometime so I can meet him," I said.

"He doesn't like lawyers."

"Oh? How come?"

"That time he ran over that nun? This lawyer his dad got really didn't have any respect for Turk. I mean, the nun wasn't even hurt much. It wasn't his fault she was so short. He just couldn't see her behind the dump truck he was backing up.''

''Turk's father owns a construction company,'' I explained to Kylie.

''Ah,'' Kylie said.

''I mean, she sprained her ankle was all,'' Jamie said. ''It wasn't like she *died* or anything.''

The horn. For the third time.

''He isn't real patient sometimes,'' Jamie explained. Then, ''Gee, I've got a lot of other stories about stuff me'n Turk did, Kylie. We'll have to get together again sometime.''

''You know,'' Kylie said, sounding sincere. ''I'd actually like that.''

Jamie was wearing a pair of jeans so tight they should be illegal. Unfair to lechers like me.

Kylie sat down in the client chair. ''She really made me feel better. She's not a genius but there's an innocence and an energy that's really great to be around.''

''Great. So you're feeling better.''

''Much better, actually. I can't believe it.''

And then her body sort of collapsed in on itself and she started sobbing. ''I've been up and down like this ever since he told me about his affair,'' she managed to say.

I didn't have any Kleenex so I went into the can and got several fistfuls of toilet paper.

She said, when she'd gathered herself, ''I should leave him, shouldn't I?''

''Oh, no.''

''Oh, no, what?''

''No advice. You give people advice on matters of the heart, you lose them as friends forever.''

"But I'm *asking* for advice. That absolves you of all responsibility."

"You say that now—but later..."

"C'mon, McCain. You really think I should leave him, don't you?"

I took her hand in mine and gently said, "You know what I really think?"

"What?"

"That we should go get some lunch."

She jerked her hand away. "Coward."

"Damn right I'm a coward. I have three fewer friends today because I advised them on their affairs of the heart. They won't speak to me. Now, let's go."

THE WADING POOL in the town square was packed with tots. You could hear them squealing, summer music on a summer breeze. There was a drowsy, siesta feeling such as you always read about in the western novels of Mr. Max Brand, for whom I'd formed a real affection. I'd read two of his when I was twelve and then kept on reading. His heroes were always brooders and mourners and failures and daydreamers and that lent his stories a uniqueness and depth most westerns just don't have, John Wayne forgive me. He was especially great at describing Mexico. And that, at least in my imagination, was how our little town felt at this noontime. Some dusty Mexican pueblo where this really neat-looking short guy rides in on a white horse and all the señoritas come running. It was so hot here today tires were losing tread simply by revolving against the steamy pavement.

Kylie spotted them before I did. On the windshield of a pink-and-white Nash rambler. And on the windshield of a nice new Pontiac convertible. And on the window of a Dairy Queen panel truck.

Flyers.

She snatched one up. Glanced at it. Flicked it in my face.

WHY THE JEWS WANT JFK TO WIN!

THE ZIONIST POWERS BEHIND THE KEN-NEDYS!

The rest you can imagine for yourself.

"But didn't old man Kennedy hang around with Hit-ler?" she asked.

"Liked the man very much. Considered him a friend. That's one of the reasons the Kennedys have to keep old Joe out of sight. A lot of people still resent the old bastard."

"Then why do they think the Jews are behind Ken-nedy?"

"I guess I don't know," I said. "Maybe for the same reasons the Jews are stashing all their guns in church basements."

"These people are *nuts!*" she said with great au-thority. "As my folks always pointed out."

Her folks were (a) university professors and (b) Jew-ish, in a time when it was not universally fashionable to be either. Kylie'd grown up in Madison, Wisconsin, one of the most lovely and exciting cities in the U.S.

"Well, they get to economize on this election any-way," I said.

We started walking again. She started fanning her-self with her fingers. She had wonderful long fingers. Artistic, I guess you'd say. She also had a very artistic ass.

"How are they economizing?"

"Well, when the Klan and the other crazies get all

riled up around election time, they usually take the
Jews and the Catholics on separately. But since Kennedy has a lot of Jewish advisers, they've decided they
can save on their printing bills by doubling up. The
only thing they didn't get to is the Eleanor-Roosevelt-
is-a-lesbo-thing.''

"Eleanor Roosevelt is a lesbian?''

"That's what all the pamphlets say. Say, I wonder
if Kenny Thibodeau has heard that one. There's a political novel in it for him. *Lesbo Legislators*.''

She laughed. "He's actually an interesting guy.''

"Yeah, he is.''

"He goes away to all these big cities and comes
back and tells us what's going on. You know, trends,
and stuff. I even read a couple of his novels.''

"Shameless hussy,'' I said.

"He can write people well. I was surprised. I asked
him why he doesn't write a serious book and you know
what he told me?''

"What?''

"He said that every time he tries, he freezes up.
Blocks. But that he can write his porno just fine because he knows it's just trash and doesn't matter. I sort
of feel sorry for him.''

"You feel sorry for everybody.''

"Look who's talking.''

AL MONAHAN HAS two bus-stop benches on either side
of the entrance to his café. Nice for eating outdoors on
hot days, which we did. I had iced tea and a cheeseburger. She had iced tea.

"I thought you wanted some lunch.''

"Iced tea is lunch,'' she said defensively.

"I'd hate to hear you argue that in court.''

"Want to take the case?"

"You should eat," I said.

"You should stop being a mother hen."

"That's the most effective diet in the world. Heart-break."

"It sure is."

"When's the last time you ate?"

"Last night. A piece of pizza."

I was about to do a little more mother-henning when I saw them.

Sara and Dierdre Hall. Jaywalking from the other side of the street.

"Be right back," I said and jumped up, setting my lunch down.

I caught them just as they reached their baby-blue DeSoto convertible. They were dressed pretty much the same—pink summer blouses, white pedal pushers, white dressy sandals. And the darkest sunglasses this side of Elizabeth Taylor. They looked alike, too. Quiet beauty all the richer the longer you studied it.

"Hi, Sara, I wondered if I could call you this afternoon."

"Get in the car, Dierdre."

"Mom, didn't you hear him?"

"Didn't you hear *me*, Dierdre? I said to get in the car."

"Sara, we really do need to sit down and talk."

"Mom, do you have any idea how embarrassing this is? Why don't you at least answer him?"

"I'll answer him when you get in the car."

"This is very embarrassing, Mr. McCain. I'm sorry."

"It's all right. Your mom's obviously having a bad day."

"My mom's *always* having a bad day."

Dierdre got in the car. Crossed her arms across her chest.

"I have nothing to say to you," Sara Hall said to me.

"I'm trying to help you, Sara."

"How noble."

"Would you prefer if I just started talking right here? In front of your daughter?"

"Yes, Mother," Dierdre said. "That'd be fun, wouldn't it?"

"I resent this," Sara Hall said.

"So do I. You owe me some answers."

"I don't owe you anything. And I plan to take this up with Judge Whitney, believe me."

I knew better than to say that the Judge already knew I'd be talking to Sara. "I'd appreciate it if you'd be at my office at four o'clock."

"If she isn't there, *I* will be, Mr. McCain."

That was another point I'd make on my list. Muldaur's daughter and Hall's daughter offering to cooperate even though their mothers refused to.

"I'll see you at four," Sara Hall said, and got into her car.

I could see them pantomiming an argument as the swept-fin convertible swept away. I had the sense that it was an argument they'd had many times. I wondered what it was about. I felt sure it had some bearing on the murders.

"Ah," I said, sitting down next to Kylie on the bench again and picking up my lunch. "Just the way I like it. My cheeseburger's cold and my iced tea's hot."

"I'm now a black-belt in fly-shooing. It looked like

Pearl Harbor on your burger.'' She sipped her iced tea.
''So, did you learn anything?''

''Just that Sara and Dierdre Hall don't seem to get
along very well.''

''Any idea why?''

''Not yet.''

''Meaning you plan to find out?''

''Of course. Before Richard Milhous Nixon gets
here and finds out that we have murders just like everybody else.''

''He says he's not sure if he loves her.''

''I take it we're not talking about Nixon anymore.''

''He says he knows he's being unfair to me and he
wouldn't blame me if I just walked out. We really got
into a terrible argument—the people downstairs were
banging on the wall and everything—and then we
ended up making love practically all night. And then
when he was leaving for school this morning—even
though he doesn't have any classes today—I asked him
if I'd see him tonight and he said that he had a date
with her.''

''Ah.''

''That's all you're going to say? Ah? What kind of
comment is that?''

''A non-comment. I'm staying out of this, remember?''

''Well, pretend it's you and not me. What would
you do, then?''

''That's how it sorta was at the end with Pamela.
We finally made love one night and as soon as we were
finished the phone rang. It was good ole Stu and she
went rushing off to him.''

''Really?''

''Yeah.''

"Did you take her back?"

"She never came back. Not really, anyway. She snuck away a few days later because Stu was having second thoughts about dumping his wife and family and the governorship."

"What governorship?"

"Everybody figured it was his turn to be governor."

"But he's here now."

"Yes, he is. Rebuilding his image after running away with a hussy."

"And where's Pamela?"

"Hiding somewhere. I'm not sure where, exactly."

"What if she called and asked you to get married?"

"I don't know. That's the only answer I can give you."

"She walked all over you."

"Yes."

"And ditched you for somebody else."

"Yes."

"And you'd still consider taking her back."

"I'd consider it, I suppose."

"Well, that's exactly how I'd feel, McCain. I'd consider it."

"We're a couple of fools," I said, "is what we are."

"Damned fools."

"Double-damned fools."

"We're really pathetic, you know that?"

"Do I know it? Do I know it? I make myself sick I know it so much."

And that's when I saw this guy working his way up the street, slipping leaflets under windshield wipers.

"I'll call you at work this afternoon," I said.

"I'm really going to need you tonight, McCain."

"Good. Because I'm really going to need you, too."

She grabbed my hand. "You are?"

"Sure I am." And then I did something I really shouldn't ought to have done. I leaned over and gave her a kiss right on the mouth. A married woman—well, a somewhat married woman—right on the mouth.

Just the kind of thing I'd expect from you, I could hear my ninth-grade nun, Sister Mary Florence, saying. *Just the kind of thing I'd expect from you.*

ELEVEN

JOHN PARNELL WAS a chunky guy with a limp that resulted from a grade-school tractor accident. He wore a lime-colored T-shirt and jeans and sandals. He was bending over a Ford station wagon to slap a leaflet beneath its windshield.

"Hi, John."

He backed himself off the car hood he'd been bent over and said, "Hey, McCain, how ya doin'?"

"Fine. Or I was till I saw you putting those leaflets on car windows."

He grinned. "Yeah, that'd make the nuns mad, wouldn't it?"

I nodded to the stack of leaflets in his car. He was still the freckled, snub-nosed guy I'd always known. I couldn't connect him to the leaflets.

"You printed them and now you're distributing them?"

"Yep. That's what God wants me to do, McCain."

"He told you that?"

"Now you're being blasphemous, Sam."

Maybe this wasn't the old Parnell I'd known.

"You're a Catholic, Parnell, and you're handing this stuff out?"

He shook his head. "Not anymore I'm not. A Catholic, I mean."

"Since when?"

He shrugged. "Well, the wife—I'm not sure you ever met her, gal from Sioux City I met when I was doing my printing apprenticeship up there—anyway, she was raised as an evangelical. And what with one thing and another she kinda got me interested in the whole thing. She always says you should feel bad when you go to church. And I tried 'em all—Lutheran, Baptist, Presbyterian. But they always tried to make you feel good. But bad's the only way you know your religion's workin' for you. When you feel terrible. And that's what we both liked about Reverend Muldaur. His whole deal was how unworthy we all are. And I believe that, McCain. You might believe something else—but that's what *I* believe, McCain."

"But the snakes—"

"That's what people don't understand."

"What don't people understand?"

"They're not snakes."

"They sure looked like it to me."

"They're devils. Really and truly. Devils. Evil spirits. I've held them. I can feel their evil. I truly can. But they didn't bite me because Reverend Muldaur cleansed my soul before he handed me the snakes."

"But all this bullshit about Jews and Catholics—"

"I don't use words like b.s. anymore, Sam. But I'll tell you, they're both out to conquer the world. They know they can't do it alone, so they've joined forces. And the only people who can stop them are people like me." He leaned forward confidentially. He smelled of sweat and onions. "And there're a lot of people in this town who believe the same way I do, Sam. But they don't want people to know it."

"So you just gave him all this printing free?"

ED GORMAN

119

"Heck, no. A friend of his paid for it."

"What friend?"

He leaned toward me again. He must've had an onion sandwich with some onion rings and onion juice on the side. "Like I said, Sam, there're a lot of folks in this town who agree with everything we do. And one of them was nice enough to pick up the tab for the printing. I just charged my costs. No profit. That wouldn't be right, seeing's how I was doing it for the Lord."

Parnell, Parnell, what did somebody drug you with? How can you possibly believe this crap?

Then I realized it was time for me to go pick up the rabbi and the monsignor. We were doing some target practice this afternoon with the guns in the church basement.

"I'd really appreciate it if you told me who paid for the printing, John. I'm trying to find out who killed Muldaur."

"I know you are. We all hear the judge is trying to get it all cleaned up before Nixon gets here. Now, there's a guy with almost as many Jew friends as Kennedy has. Hard to know who to vote for."

I couldn't deal with it any longer.

"You're making me so damn sad, Parnell."

"And you're making me sad, too, Sam. I saw you over there eating with that Jewess. She's not fit company for a true Christian, Sam."

"Well, she's fit company for me. She's a damned good woman, in fact."

He shook his head. He really did seem sad. "The ways of the flesh, Sam, the ways of the flesh."

AT ONE TIME, the two-room house had probably looked pretty nice sitting all alone by the fast creek in the curve of a copse of pine. It looked like one of those houses a fella could order himself from the Sears Roebuck catalog late in the 1890s. Such homes came with assembly instructions; the fancier kits even included hammers and other tools. You could see some of these Sears houses standing well into the 1940s, by the grace of spit and God, as the old saying had it.

Ned Blimes, whose last name and current address I'd learned by asking around, didn't seem to be at home as I pulled my ragtop behind a stand of pine to the west of his house. I didn't want my car to pick up any stray bullets.

A dainty man, he wasn't. His meals apparently included a lot of self-shot squirrel meat because the grass on the side of his place was strewn with carcasses. Several gleaming crows hovered nearby. I'd interrupted their meal. I've never been able to tolerate the smell of squirrel meat frying. The air was coarse and bloody with it.

I knocked on the front door of the shack-like house. The lone front window was filled with cardboard and just a jagged remnant of the glass that had once covered it.

The crows went back to eating. The pollen got to me and I sneezed. And somebody poked something in my back.

The smell told me it was Yosemite Sam himself.

"Put your hands over your head."

"This high enough?"

"Higher."

"This is as high as I can go."

"What'chu want, McCain?"

"I wanted to ask you some questions."

"About what?"

"About Muldaur."

"Don't want to talk about Muldaur."

"Why not?"

"Because that was part of the bargain."

"What bargain?"

He guffawed. Or whinnied. I couldn't be sure. Maybe it was a guffaw-whinny. "That's for me to know and you to find out."

"Gee, I haven't heard that one since third grade."

"Huh?"

"How about taking the gun out of my back?"

"Then how about you gettin' in that car of yours and gettin' the hell out of here?"

Then he started marching me back to my car.

I still had my hands above my head. There was a variety of animal poop all over the buffalo grass. I am happy to report that my black penny loafers didn't touch any of it.

"What happened out there the day you took Muldaur snakin'?"

"Who tole you somethin' happened?"

"You did."

"I did? When?"

"When I saw you at Muldaur's place. You said something like 'He was the only one who made any money that day.'"

"Shit," he said.

"What?"

"You sure I said that?"

"I sure am."

"Then I shouldnt've. Me'n my big mouth."

We'd reached my car.

He prodded and poked me with the barrel of his rifle.
I got in and got behind the wheel.

"You just forget I said anything, mister."

"I'm not going to."

"Well, you damned well better," he said.

"You can't make me."

"Bet I can," he said, and put the tip of the rifle
about three inches from my face.

"You always talk like you're in third grade?"

"Do you? Now you get the hell out of here and you
don't bother me no more, you understand that?"

WHEN I GOT back to the office, I got out my list and
added a few more items.

Why were Sara and Dierdre Hall so angry at each
other?

Who paid Parnell the printing costs?

What happened the day Muldaur and Ned Blimes
went snaking? Jamie had left me a type note:

I FINISSHED UP TYYPING EARLIE SO ME
AND TTURC WENT SWIMMING. THIS TIME
WIT OUR CLOSE ON. HE-HE. I CRACKED A
FUNNIE, MRR C. JAMIE

Well, she was coming along, anyway, God love her.
A couple of times she'd even mistyped her own
name—"Jammie" and "Jaamie"—so hanging around
Turk—excuse me "Tturc"—was apparently starting to
pay off. The first time I'd interviewed her for the job,
she'd told me, "My dad says he hasn't got a lot upstairs, Turk I mean, and maybe he doesn't. But he's
got a lot of common sense. Like one day this big dog
was really growling at me and he had this kind of

foamy stuff dripping from his mouth. And you know what Turk said? He said, 'Don't try to pet him or nothing, Jamie. He looks kinda mad.' See what I mean? He's got a lot of common sense, Mr. C.''

The Common Sense Typing Method.

A volume that should be in every school library.

Between 2:09 and 3:53 I got four calls. Two of the callers were clients explaining why they couldn't pay me this month, and two were people who wanted to sell me some things. Maybe if the first two callers came through with money, I might be able to buy things from the second two.

I looked through some court documents the county attorney had shipped me; a dunning letter from my alumni association; a copy of *Time* with Ike on the cover. The WWII people would always be my true heroes. Even a little town like ours lost twenty-eight men and women in the war. And you never forgot. Some people talked about their war experiences and some didn't. But whether they held their memories public or private, they could never let go of them. There are some things you go through that change you forever—even if you don't want to be changed—and war is one of them. My dad still has nightmares sometimes, my mom says, and they're always about his war experiences. I didn't agree with everything Ike believed politically but I admired him a damned sight more than I did showboats like Patton and MacArthur. MacArthur I gave up on when he said we should drop atomic bombs on China. He enjoyed war too much to be trusted. He loved posing against a backdrop of explosions and bombed-out people trooping down lonely roads. I always laughed about what Ike said when asked what he'd done as an Army captain in the South

Seas during the 1930s, when he'd served as MacArthur's secretary: "I studied drama under General MacArthur." MacArthur never forgave Ike for that crack.

Just before Sara Hall was due, my dad called and said, "Don't forget Monday's your mom's birthday."

"God, I'm glad you reminded me."

"She says she doesn't want us to make a big deal of it. But you know better and so do I."

"Mind if I bring somebody new? And she's not a date exactly. Kylie Burke."

"That newspaper girl? She's sure a cutie. And nice, too. She interviewed a bunch of us at the VFW last year. Sure, bring her."

"Maybe Kylie can help me pick out a gift, too."

"Well, I'm goin' fishin', son. Talk to you later."

Four-fifteen and Sara Hall still hadn't appeared. I picked up the phone book, found her number, dialed it. No answer.

Four twenty-one. A timid knock.

"Yes?"

"It's Dierdre Hall, Mr. McCain."

"C'mon in."

She was dressed as she had been earlier, but her shades were pushed back on her head.

"Where's your mom?"

"I—I'm not sure."

"Boy, are you lousy at it."

"At what?"

"Lying. Your entire face is red."

"Oh, shit."

"C'mon in and sit down and let's talk."

"I'm sorry I lied."

"It's all right. Just sit down. We can talk about your

mom later. What I want to know for now is why *you* decided to come over.''

She hesitated a long time. ''My mom's going to kill me for coming here.''

''Let's worry about that later.''

She scanned my office for gremlins, a pretty girl with more poise than one would expect in somebody her age. That was my thought, anyway. But then she sort of spoiled the impression by jerking up from her chair, covering her mouth with her hand—the way I always did when the Falstaff beer started backing up— and rushed out the door to the john on the other side of the coatrack.

My charm had worked once again on a female. They didn't usually go so far as to barf literally. Only figuratively.

The exterior door opened and Sara Hall, angry and frantic, rushed in, scanning my office much as her daughter had only moments earlier, and said, ''Where is she?''

She wore the same outfit she'd worn earlier, too, but her shades were over her eyes.

''Who?''

''I don't want any of your guff, McCain. You know who. If you don't tell me, I'll have Sykes arrest you for contributing to the delinquency of a minor. Or maybe statutory rape would be even better.''

''Why don't you sit down and quit acting crazy?''

''Where is she, McCain? I'm serious about calling Sykes.''

And then we both heard Dierdre throw up for the second time.

''Oh, Lord,'' Sara said. She didn't sound angry; she sounded drained, weary.

She came in and sat down and took off her sunglasses and then covered her face with lovely fingers.

"Sara, why don't you tell me what's going on?"

She shook her head. Said from behind her hands, "I
can't, McCain. I wish I could. I wish I could tell somebody, anyway." Then, "This is when I resent my husband dying on me. He should be here. He was stronger
than I was with things like this." Then, whispering,
"This whole thing."

I almost asked what whole thing.

"You're not weak," I said.

"No, I'm pretty strong. But this whole thing—"

We were back to the this-whole-thing thing.

Toilet flushing. Water running. Paper towel being
cinched free from the dispenser. Door opening.

She came up to the door and said, "Mom!"

Sara turned in her chair as if she'd been shot.

"How'd you know I'd be here?"

"You told me you trusted McCain, remember? So
when you snuck away this was the first place I thought
of."

"I didn't tell him anything, if that's what you're
worried about."

Sara seemed ecstatic. "Really?"

"Really, Mom."

Then to me: "Really? She didn't—?"

I shook my head. "Didn't have time. Started to.
Then got sick."

Sara was as bad at lying as Dierdre. "She's been
sick—the flu—"

"We're way down the road on that one, Sara," I
said.

"I don't know what that means." Sounding scared.

"It means she's pregnant. That's why she was throwing up."

Sara gasped the way women in movies gasp. Dierdre showed no particular expression.

"Then you *did* tell him!" Sara snapped, crazed again.

"Mom, he figured it out. Throwing up in the middle of the day. Me coming over here to tell him some kind of secret. You being so wound-up and all—he figured it out for himself."

Sara turned to me again. "Please don't tell anybody, McCain. Please promise me."

My seventeen-year-old sister had gotten pregnant a few years ago. People still whispered about her, snickered, even after she'd fled to Chicago. Nobody deserved that kind of treatment.

"Don't worry, Sara. I won't say a word."

"I have to trust you, McCain."

"I know." I reached over and took her hand. "And you can." To her daughter, I said, "How about taking ole Mom home and helping her relax?"

Sara smiled anxiously. "Ole Mom here could sure use one."

I hadn't learned anything other than that a high-school girl had gotten herself in trouble, the kind of trouble small-town gossips, lineal descendants of the folks who ran the Salem witch trials, loved to dote on. But now wasn't the time to push for anything more.

"You're a good man, McCain."

"And you're a good woman, Sara."

Sara and Dierdre hugged briefly and left.

Leaving me to wonder if her pregnancy had anything in particular to do with our two most recent murders.

TWELVE

WE ENDED UP EATING in the backyard that night with Mrs. Goldman. She'd been grilling herself a burger and so we threw our own burgers on the fire and joined her at the small picnic table.

"We tried out that new dance boat last night," Mrs. Goldman said, in between shooing away flies and slapping mosquitoes.

"How was it?" Kylie said.

"A lot of fun."

A couple of retired men had spent a year building a large, completely enclosed dance boat that was decorated like a restaurant and dance club inside. Booths lined two of the walls and there were three decks where you could stand for romantic moonlit glimpses of the night.

"How about we give it a try?" Kylie said.

"Fine," I said.

She must've seen how Mrs. Goldman was watching us.

"My husband and I are separated for the time being," Kylie said.

"It's really not any of my business."

Kylie laughed. "I don't care about my reputation. It's McCain's I'm worried about. I don't want to spoil his virginal image."

Mrs. Goldman smiled. "His life seems to have slowed down the last few months here."

"He's just resting up. He'll come roaring back."

"I really like it when people talk about you like you're not here," I said.

Kylie and I were sitting next to each other on one side of the table. Mrs. Goldman's summer garden imbued the dusk with exotic odors you don't usually associate with states where corn and pigs are economic staples. I was having my usual reaction to that purgatory between day and night, that melancholy that was not quite despair but came pretty close.

Kylie slid her arm around me. "I wouldn't have made it these last few days without Sam here."

"Ditto for her. I've been kinda down myself."

"Well, you never know where things like this will lead," Mrs. Goldman said.

Dogs barked; children laughed; a group of three very young teen couples walked down the alley, boys nervously teasing the girls they liked, not knowing what else to do, that wonderful awkward terrifying time of first love; and night, irrevocable and vast, fell upon the prairie. I wanted, for a brief firefly moment there, to be one of those teenage boys, starting all over again, wanting in some ways, what with my failed foolish pursuit of the beautiful Pamela Forrest, to start all over again, an eternal late summer of county fairs and swimming-pool dates and Saturday night movie dates.

But even at the young age of twenty-four things had become irretrievably complicated. Pamela, whom I shouldn't have loved; Mary, whom I should have; and poor sad Kylie and her strutting jerk of a husband. I really wanted to sleep with Kylie but she was married. And so I was afraid I would, against my principles;

and afraid I wouldn't, against that pure clean lust I felt
for her. She was so damned good and kind and smart
and sexy in her kid-sister way.

We all went inside and had some iced tea in Mrs.
Goldman's apartment—Kylie whispering that she
didn't want me to leave her alone just yet—and then
around nine-thirty, the fireflies thicker in the perfume-
scented night, a white kitten on the garden fence looking as if she were posing before the half moon...we
went upstairs.

"SO," KYLIE SAID, half an hour later, "what happens
if I stay here tonight?"

"I'm of two minds about that."

"I'm of three or four minds about that."

"Well, then, it looks like we have a dilemma here,
doesn't it?"

"A conundrum."

"Where's Chad tonight?"

"Whereabouts unknown."

"And you—"

"—don't feel like going through another Strindberg
play with him. Strindberg being his favorite writer. So
when we get into one of our arguments, he always
starts doing Strindberg. And I've had enough Strindberg for a while."

"You can't ever have too much Strindberg."

"You like him?"

"Eh," I said, shrugging. "In a pinch, I suppose."

"So I'll take the couch."

"You're too long for the couch."

"I'm the same size you are."

"You're always telling me," I said, "that you're
taller than I am."

"Haven't you figured out by now that I'm an incorrigible liar?"

"I'll take the couch. It'll make me feel nobler."

"I'd really feel awkward doing that to you."

"You'd deprive me of feeling noble?"

"It's still pretty early. Could we watch a little TV?"

"But of course."

We started out watching "Highway Patrol." Broderick Crawford never takes off his trench coat. They could have deep-sea sequences like on "Sea Hunt" with Lloyd Bridges and Brod would still be wearing his trench coat, his Aqua-Lung strapped on outside of it. Oh, and he'd be wearing his fedora, too.

I say "started out watching" because, after about one act of ole Brod barking "Ten-four, ten-four" into his two-way, we gave up and started making out.

I guess we resolved our dilemma and our conundrum.

At least sort of.

It was ninth-grade sex.

We French-kissed but when my hand drooped (of its own volition) toward her chest area (or chestal area as Judge Ronald D. K. M. Sullivan would say), it was gently moved back up by her hand.

By the time "Highway Patrol" was wrapping up we lay lengthwise on the couch. Pressed very tightly together. She was a great kisser. Maybe the best kisser I'd ever been with. She was such a great kisser that kissing her was almost enough. But my hand kept drooping and her hand kept gently brushing it away. We did a little tenth-grade dry-humping but she wouldn't let my hand linger on her bottom. I had one of those erections that make you crazy. One of those erections that takes you over so completely you are nothing more than a penis.

She was girl-flesh and girl-body and girl-mouth; girl-sigh, girl-gasp, girl-moan.

She was moaning, I was moaning.

She was insinuating (a Kenny Thibodeau dirty-book word) herself against me as hard and fast as I was insinuating myself against her.

I suppose in the murky past I'd wanted the beautiful Pamela Forrest this badly but it was really murky. Nobody had ever seemed as fresh and vital and fetching as Kylie did right now.

And then she was up and grabbing her purse and rushing out the door.

"I've got to get out of here!" she said. "I don't want to do anything I'd regret. Good-night, McCain! I'm sorry!"

AT SEVEN-THIRTY the following morning I sat in my ragtop on a shelf of shale above the cup of grassy land where the hill folk lived. My field binoculars were trained on the Muldaur trailer behind the church. At 7:47, Viola came out with a magazine and a roll of toilet paper in her hand and headed for the outhouse to the east. How'd you like to face the outhouse every morning? Summer would be bad enough—but Iowa winter when it was twenty-five below zero?

She didn't go back to the trailer till 8:24.

Daughter Ella carrying, presumably, the same roll of t.p. but a different magazine, emerged from the trailer at 8:48 and went to the outhouse. She stayed only till 9:03.

At 9:26 I got the opportunity I'd been waiting for. Viola got in the rusty truck and drove away, leaving

Ella behind. I drove down to the trailer and walked up to the door.

The place smelled of decades-old grime. The yard was spiked with broken glass, empty bottles, rusty cans. A TV turned low hummed in the front wall.

I knocked.

As I waited for a response, I turned to look at the land behind the church. I wondered how thoroughly Cliffie and his minions had searched the area of weeds and buffalo grass and the four rusty garbage cans.

I turned back to the trailer when I heard the door open but by then it was too late. The angry man had his shotgun pointed at me. Bib overalls, T-shirt beneath, massive head, shoulders, forearms.

"C'mon," he said.

He was the keeper of the gate. The man who'd let Kylie and me into the church that first night. The man arguing with his wife a little later on, striking her.

"What's your name, anyway?"

"You think I'm afraid to tell you? It's Bill Oates."

"What's with the shotgun, Mr. Oates?"

"I want to take you somewhere."

"I came here to see Ella."

"Ella don't want to see you."

"It'd probably be better if I heard that from her myself."

"We suffered a loss. You don't seem to understand that. You shouldn't be botherin' people at a time like this. If you was pure, you wouldn't be."

"How do you know I'm not pure?"

"You work for that Judge, for one thing. And I'm told you're going around with that Jew woman."

"And that makes me impure?"

He smiled and for the first time I saw the stubby blackened teeth. "I guess we're going to find out, ain't we?"

YOU'RE PROBABLY AHEAD of me on this one. Not even when he marched me over to the church at gunpoint did I realize what he had in mind. Slow learner, I guess.

The church interior was shadowy. The chairs were arranged in orderly fashion. The altar was dark.

On a hot day like this all the ancient service-station odors rose up. You could almost hear the bell on the drive clanging to life and a motorist saying, "Fill 'er up, would ya? And I guess you'd better check the oil."

And then I heard them. And then I had my first understanding—dread, actually—of why he'd brought me here. And the real implication of his "pure" remark.

He nudged me down the aisle with the barrel of his gun.

I began to make out the dimensions of the snake cage. I tried to guess from their sudden hissing and rattling—the approach of intruders—how many of them there were.

"What the hell you going to do?"

"Just keep walkin'."

I stopped. In an instant I weighed the threat—getting shot in the back versus having to do something with rattlesnakes. So I stopped.

He stabbed the barrel of the shotgun nearly all the way through me.

"I said to keep walkin'."

"I'm not going near those damned snakes."

"Watch your language. This is the house of the Lord."

"And I suppose the Lord wants you to put those snakes on me?"

"You're not pure."

I flung myself forward, hitting the floor and rolling to the right. I was slower than I'd hoped and he was much, much faster.

He put a bullet about three inches from my head. It ripped up some concrete and ricocheted off the far shadowy wall. You could smell the gunfire; the rattle of it echoed in the small place.

"Get up."

He came over and kicked my ankle so hard it felt broken.

"You bastard."

He kicked me again in the same place. Even harder.

"The next time you use a word like that, I'll put a bullet in your brain."

The bullet or the snake? They each frightened me but in different ways. At least a bullet didn't have those glassy eyes and those fangs and that forked tongue and that—

But I got to my feet. I didn't want to die on the floor there. Got to my feet and tried to stand tall but it was difficult and not just because I'm short. It was difficult because my right ankle hurt so much where he'd kicked me.

He grabbed me by the shoulder and flung me on the altar.

There had to be at least three of them, maybe four. They made even more noise than the bullet had. Angry, filthy noise.

I stumbled on the altar platform and sprawled face-down before the small raised box on top of which the snake cage sat.

"Stand up."

"What're you going to do?"

"You said you were pure! I'll give you the chance to prove it."

"I'm not going to handle those snakes."

"I'm sick of talk, you. Now stand up."

The pain in my ankle was fading much faster than I had thought possible. But I didn't want him to kick me again. This time he'd probably break bone.

"I'm not afraid of the snakes because I'm true to my Lord."

"Is that why you slapped your wife the night Muldaur died? Because the Lord wanted you to?"

"He's ordained that sometimes man needs to instruct woman in the ways of righteousness."

"And that includes slapping them around?"

"I don't take any pleasure in it, if that's what you mean. I do it because the Lord has ordained it. I'd be committing a sin if I *didn't* do it."

All the time the hissing continued.

"Sometimes one man must instruct another man in the ways of righteousness, too."

"That's what you're doing with me?"

"You need to know if you're impure. I'm actually doin' you a favor."

"Gosh, thanks so much."

He prodded me with his toe just above the ankle. I really didn't want to get kicked again. I pushed myself to my feet.

Sometimes, you kid yourself and think you're tough. But then something like this happens. I'd banged my head on the floor just now and had a headache. My ankle was sore. I was pasty with sweat. And all I could hear were the snakes.

I was being pushed toward them. They may not actually have been louder, they may not actually have been angrier. But they sure sounded that way. I stumbled toward them.

He clubbed me on the side of the head hard with his rifle barrel.

I dropped to my knees before I realized where I'd be: kneeling next to the snake cage.

"Open it up."

He had to shout to be heard above the hiss and rattle.

I just looked at him. Terrible things were going on in my throat, my chest, my bowels.

"You open that up and grab one of 'em. If it don't bite you then you are judged worthy by Divine Wisdom."

I couldn't talk. Literally. I tried. But my throat was raw and dry with fear. Only a few inches and a mesh of metal kept the rattlers at bay.

I wondered if he'd really shoot me. He seemed crazed but was he *that* crazed? And—a wild thought that should have occurred to me much earlier—what had he been doing in the Muldaur trailer so early in the morning? He'd arrived before I had. What was his exact relationship to Viola Muldaur? Was *he* pure? Could *he* pass the snake test?

Then he did it. Leaned in, unlatched the simple lock that held the lid down on the cage.

"I'm makin' it easy for you."

And for the second time, he fired his weapon.

One year at camp I'd slept in the grass and during the night a bat kept flying inches over my face. I always remembered the heat of its passage. The bullet was like that now. The heat of its passage.

I did a kind of dance on my knees, jerking sideways,

frontways, slamming into the snake cage. And then doing, in simple animal reaction, the unthinkable.

I reached my arm out and grabbed the far side of the cage to keep it from falling off the low table it was resting on. And then I jerked back, astonished at my stupidity as the snakes flew out at me, at least two snakes arcing their heads into the top of the cage, trying to get at me.

"Open it!" Oates shouted.

And then swung the rifle barrel into the side of my head again. My entire consciousness was sliding into pain. It was getting difficult for me to think. I nudged up against the cage.

He swung the rifle around yet another time.

This time I consciously stopped myself from bumping against the cage.

And this time I realized how I could get out of this situation, rifle or no rifle.

It was not without risk. There would be a few seconds there when the snakes would be close to me, able to bite me and hold on if they wanted to. But I didn't have much choice. The snakes or the religious crackpot—you decide.

"Open it," he said. His voice was raw now. He'd glimpsed the future. One of the snakes striking me, filling me with poison. He spoke in the raspy tone of true passion.

So I opened it.

But I kept hold of the handle to the lid. And instead of shoving my hand inside, I used the handle to swing the entire cage around and fling it at him.

He screamed like a young boy.

He fired two shots.

And he dropped his gun when one of the flying rattlers slapped him across the face.

The gun discharged when it hit the floor.

I was already halfway down the aisle, my sore ankle be damned, heading for my ragtop.

THIRTEEN

I WENT HOME AND took a very cold shower. I stood in there fifteen minutes trying to get snake off me. Part of it was psychological, of course. You couldn't scrub away a sense of snake. It stayed with you for a long, long time.

I'd just finished getting into some clean summer-weight clothes—white short-sleeved shirt, blue-on-blue striped necktie, blue slacks, black socks, black loafers—when the phone rang.

"You're going to think I'm crazy."

"He called and said that he still loved you."

"Yeah, sort of, anyway."

"So you're going to see him."

"Tonight. That's why I called. I told him I was with you last night and I think he got jealous. He started insisting that we get together tonight."

"You know something?"

"What?"

"I'd do the same thing you would. I'd go."

"Really?"

"Are you kidding? Look at all the times I went running back to Pamela."

"Yeah, I guess you were kind of a glutton for punishment."

"Well, as one glutton to another, why not give it a try?" I said.

"You think it might actually lead somewhere?"

"Probably not," I said. "But it's nice to have a little hope again, isn't it?"

"Hearing 'maybe' is always better than hearing 'no.'"

"That's right," I said.

"Even if 'maybe' is a lie?"

I sighed. "Yeah, kiddo, even if 'maybe' is a lie."

"You're really a wise man, McCain. You should run for pope or something."

"I was thinking of that. I'd like to wear that hat he does. You know that really tall one? With the lifts I have in my shoes, that hat would make me seven feet."

She laughed. "Thanks for being such a good friend."

"My pleasure."

Pause. "I really did want to sleep with you last night."

"Same here."

"Chad's the only guy I've ever slept with, though. So it would've been a really big step."

"I understand. I'm running for pope, remember?"

MRS. COURTNEY WAS just leaving the two-story, red-brick Colonial-style rectory when I pulled up. She wore a black suit on this boiling day. She had the look and air of a millionaire's wife, a somewhat lacquered and severe middle-aged blonde who did not belong out here in the sticks. Attractive but not appealing. As if money—or in her case, the prestige of Harvard Divinity—had bled all the juices out of her. I reached her just before she got into her dark-blue Chrysler.

"Mrs. Courtney, my name is—"

"I know who you are, Mr. McCain. I hope you'll excuse me but I'm in a hurry. I need to be at the mortuary in five minutes." Her voice was cool if not quite cold. No reading on her eyes. Shades.

"I'd really appreciate ten minutes of your time."

"For what, Mr. McCain?" The words weren't slurred. But they were slightly indistinct. Or was I imagining it? It had now been a few hours since the snake cage but every few moments snake images filled my mind, daymares, skewing my hold on present reality.

"I need to talk to you about your husband."

"I repeat, Mr. McCain, for what?"

Only then did I realize that she swayed slightly as she stood there, and only then did I catch the first wisps of gin aroma. Nothing else smells like gin. Praise the Lord.

"I'm trying to find out who killed him."

"So is Mr. Sykes. And he told me about half an hour ago that he's got some very promising leads."

I had to be careful here. I owed her the deference one normally gives a widow. But she was way too bright to believe that Cliffie could find a murderer. Or his ass with both hands and a compass.

"Every once in a while, he arrests the wrong person."

"He assures me that the person he has in mind is indeed the guilty party."

"Did he say who that person is?"

She put a slender hand on the door handle. Her knees gave a little, the way a drunk's do when he's been standing erect too long in one place. "Good day to you, Mr. McCain."

"Do you really want your husband's killer found, Mrs. Courtney?"

"What a ridiculous thing to say."

"If you're serious about finding his killer, you're not going to leave it up to Cliffie."

"Should I share your sentiments with him?"

"He knows my sentiments."

"You're being stupid, Mr. McCain. Why wouldn't I want my husband's killer found? I loved my husband."

"Loved him enough to protect him even after he's dead? Maybe there's something you're hiding, Mrs. Courtney."

She said, "There's a wake tonight in his honor. I need to get ready for that. And I've spent enough time with you."

I put a hand on her arm. Carefully. "This isn't any of my business, Mrs. Courtney, but are you sure you're all right to drive?"

"You're right, Mr. McCain, it isn't any of your business."

She got in her car and let the heavy door slam. She started the engine, then started the radio—classical music—and then started the air-conditioner. She swept away in a great Harvard Divinity moment.

MY COUSIN SLIM works at the state-run liquor store. There's a push on—there's been a push on for years—to get liquor by the drink in Iowa and to make bottled liquor available in a variety of retail stores...but you know how it is with conservative legislators. They're always accusing liberals of wanting to legislate morality—especially with civil rights—but they don't have any problem telling you when and where you can buy liquor, whom you can have sex with (technically, adultery is still punishable by jail time), and what you can read (they get to decide what's objectionable). Excuse the political message here. But I get irritable every time I enter a state-run liquor store. It's like getting a note from your mom telling you it's all right to have a highball:

Slim is a Korean War veteran who had one burning-bright dream the whole time he was getting his ass shot at in the snow over there. He wanted to go to work for Uncle Sam once he got done fighting for Uncle Sam. I remember the college year I spent reading most of Chekhov's stories. I just got hooked. Nobody ever wrote so well about the civil-servant mentality, and God knows, if there's one country that has that mentality, it's Mother Russia. Slim Hanrahan also has that mentality. He's a slender, gray, balding man with yellow teeth and surprisingly lively blue eyes. His favorite size in everything is small. A tiny Nash for a car, a tiny tract house for a home, a tiny woman for a wife. When he's in his cups, he always pats his flat belly and says, "Yessir, the way I figure it, I got it made. They say millionaires got it made. But they don't. You got money like that, you're always worryin' you're gonna lose it. The way I see it, the people who got it made got government jobs. You really got to be a screw-up to lose a civil-service job. And then you got the right to appeal it, anyway. There'll never be liquor-by-the-drink in this state, so I got a job for life. Reasonable hours, nothing heavy to lift, good insurance plan absolutely free. And no layoffs. Those factory guys always braggin' about how much they make an hour…but lookit how often they get laid off. Or go on strike. I've got it knocked."

That's Slim.

I decided to check with Slim since he works the day shift in our one and only liquor store. Mrs. Courtney's state of intoxication had made me curious.

"You ever see her in here?"

Slim fingered the clip-on bow tie he always wore. Another man was running the counter. "I don't know if I should be talking to you about this stuff, Sammy."

He always called me Sammy. I hated it.

"This is a murder investigation, Slim."

"You think she did it?"

'No, but I think she's acting awfully strange for a woman whose husband has just been killed."

"Oh, yeah? Funny how?"

"You think Cliffie could solve a murder?"

He shone his yellow teeth at me. "Are you kiddin'? That idiot?"

"Well, she's leaving it all up to him, she says. She's too smart for that. Which makes me wonder if there's maybe something she doesn't want to come out about her husband."

"I see what you mean. By the way, you going to the reunion this year?"

"Probably."

"My old lady and Joanie O'Hara got into it the other night at the bowling alley. So I'm kinda nervous about goin'. You notice how the O'Haras think they're a big deal since Wayne was made a foreman at the plant?"

"I guess not."

"The first thing he did was get an extension phone. They have two phones now."

"Gosh."

"Their house is even smaller than ours and they got two phones. That's what I mean, they walk around actin' like they're some sort of big deal. The wife said something about that new discount store out on the highway. This was when they got into it at the bowling alley. And you know what Joanie says?''

"What?''

"She says 'I wouldn't be seen goin' into a place like that.' Like she's too high and mighty to save a little money on stuff.''

This sounded like a matter for the United Nations if I'd ever heard one.

"Slim, you think we could get back to Mrs. Courtney?''

"Oh, yeah. Sure.''

"So does she come in here and buy liquor?''

"Now she does.''

"Now?''

"Yeah, startin' about four months ago. It was funny. Never saw her in here before. And then all of a sudden she starts comin' two, three times a week.''

"Two or three times a week. Isn't that a lot?''

"It's a lot for what she was buyin'. Half-gallon of gin at a time.''

"Was she ever drunk when she came in?''

"Not drunk but drinkin'. Slurring her words, stuff like that.''

"Hey, Slim,'' the man running the first register said, "I could use some help over here.''

The place had filled up suddenly.

"I appreciate it, Slim. Thanks.''

"I'll bet at the reunion Joanie goes around tellin' everybody about their new extension phone. Whaddaya bet?''

He went over and greeted his customer.

I DROVE OUT to the Judge's place, something I don't often do. The house is a huge Tudor set upon three acres of perfectly kept grounds that are safe behind a black iron fence. When her Eastern friends visit—I met Henry Cabot Lodge, Jr. there one day; Nelson Rockefeller and Jacob Javits another—the west lawn is covered with a vast tent, a six-piece classical ensemble, and enough booze to get Moscow drunk on a Saturday night.

The props were just now being set up as I aimed my ragtop up the curving drive to the manse. I saw Lettie and Max and Maria, the regular staff, carrying armloads of serving bowls, glasses, cups from the house to the tent. The florist was there, as was the caterer, as were the musicians. Jay Gatsby would envy what was being set in motion here.

The judge herself was in her study, Gauloise and brandy in hand. You rarely saw her in jeans, but jeans she wore and a white silk blouse. She was a little bit Rosalind Russell and a little bit Barbara Stanwyck. She was also a little bit drunk.

"So nice of you to keep me informed, McCain."

The study had one of those floor-mounted globes that was about half the size of the actual planet and walls and walls of paintings and photos of her Whitney forebears, all of whom looked constipated and skunk-mean. There was also a lot of leather furniture that smelled of a recent oiling. She also smelled, as usual, of a recent oiling.

I wasn't up for her sarcasm. "You want to hear about how I almost got my head shoved into a cage of rattlesnakes or not?"

That shut her up. Who could resist hearing a story like that? She was giddy as a girl listening to my tale of bravery and grace under pressure and which, I had to admit, I did embellish a tad here and there, especially the part about how I tied two rattlers together.

"You tied them together?"

"You bet I did. Otherwise they would've jumped on me."

"No offense, McCain, but I've just never thought of you as being that smart."

"Thank you."

"Or that brave, for that matter."

"Thank you again."

"Let me toast you."

She toasted me. You'll notice she didn't offer me a drink so that *I* could toast me.

"Ah," she said, downing the brandy. "And you learned what, exactly, for all your travail with those damnable snakes?"

"I learned that I'm much smarter and braver than you thought I was."

"You shouldn't brag, McCain. It's unbecoming."

"And I learned that Bill Oates seems to be on exceptionally good terms with Viola Muldaur." I told her about how early he'd been there this morning.

She said, delicately, "Dierdre keeps telling me that Sara isn't home and will call me back."

"Avoiding you?"

"What else?"

"I thought you were friends."

"Best of," she said.

"And she won't talk to you?"

"Afraid not."

"So she knows something."

"Afraid so," she said.

"And could be in trouble?"

"Maybe."

I told her about the mother-daughter visit to my office and about how they went home on friendly terms. And then I said, "Dierdre's pregnant. I promised her I wouldn't tell you and I probably shouldn't have. But you need to know."

"She's pregnant? But she's just a little girl."

She nearly choked inhaling the smoke from her Gauloise.

"Knocked up."

"Please, McCain. You're vulgar enough just standing there. You don't need to enhance it."

"With child. In a maternal way. Preggers, as our British friends say." She was something of an Anglophile. I thought maybe she'd go for it.

"Poor Sara," she said.

"Poor Dierdre."

"And no idea who the father is?"

"Not so far."

"Probably some greasy-haired high-school boy who drives around with his car radio turned all the way up. Like you, in fact, McCain."

"Thank you for the third time today."

"No wonder she doesn't want to talk to me." Then: "Are you any closer to figuring this thing out than you were before?"

"Not so's you'd notice."

"Then what do I pay you for, McCain? You're my investigator—investigate, for God's sake. Don't sit here soaking up my brandy and wasting my time."

"You haven't offered me any brandy."

"Oh."

"And as far as wasting your time goes, I thought you'd appreciate being brought up to date."

She went to the window and swept a graceful arm toward the grounds.

"You maybe have noticed all the activity out there."

"I did indeed."

"Dick will be here very soon."

"I'm trying to hide my enthusiasm so as not to embarrass myself."

"I want him to be comfortable here and to think well of us. I don't want him to think that we're a bunch of hill people who throw snakes around in our religious ceremonies. And murder each other."

"You'll have your killer."

"You promise?"

"I promise."

A knock at the door.

"Yes?"

Max, the butler. "There seems to be some trouble with the lilies, Judge."

"The lilies?"

"They're lagging."

"The lilies are lagging?"

"That's what the floral man says, Your Honor."

"Florist, not floral man, Max."

"The florist says the lilies are lagging, Judge. He'd like you to join him in the tent."

After Max was gone, the Judge, obviously unhappy, said, "Did you hear that, McCain?"

"I certainly did. Your lilies are lagging."

"I pay this kind of money and they lag."

"I don't want to live in a world like this anymore."

"You're more sarcastic than usual today, McCain. And since you don't seem to have any sensitivity toward my lilies, I may as well be honest with you."

"Honest? About what?"

"That ridiculous story you made up about tying two rattlesnakes together."

"You didn't believe it?"

"Not for a second."

"Well," I said as I left, "it's a hell of a lot more interesting than lagging lilies, I'll tell you that much."

FOURTEEN

ON MAIN STREET, SITTING primly on a bench in front of the Dairy Queen, I saw Kylie Burke and I almost pulled in and talked to her. But she looked so happy just then and I imagined her head was filled with all sorts of hopes and blissful fantasies about her life ahead with Chad. It's funny how love can do that to you like nothing else. You put your hand on fire just once and you know enough never to do it again. But you listen to the same person make the same empty promises again and again, and you still come back. And back. And back. And there's always the friend who knows the couple (they always live in Des Moines or Cleveland or somewhere like that) that went through exactly the same thing you're going through—all the bunco and pain and humiliation and degradation—and you know what? It was worth it because today these two are The Happiest Couple In The World. They have seventy-three children and eighteen dogs and eleven cats and they live on love. They don't need groceries, they don't need cars, they don't need baths. Who needs that stuff when you've got Love, and we're talking capital-letter Love here, of course. So maybe if you can just hang in there just a little longer you'll be exactly like this couple—maybe just like Debbie Reynolds and Eddie Fisher who look, I have to say, as if they're living on Love for sure—and then all this suffering and shame and emotional sucker-punching will be well worth it. She was probably thinking stuff like that. Because that's the sort of thing I used to think about the beautiful Pamela Forrest when she'd give me just enough hope to hang on for another couple weeks. But in the end it's us, isn't it? We could walk away anytime if we had the pride or common sense we should have. And yet we cling and hope. And have those happy-scared moments like the one Kylie was probably having now when the object of our affection throws us another sunny bit of hoke and hope.

A visitor waited for me in my client's chair.

When he turned around, I said, "*Lesbo Lummoxes.* About really lazy lesbians."

"Not bad," he said.

"I was kidding."

"Gee, McCain, so was I. I suggest a title like *Lesbo Lummoxes,* the editor probably wouldn't ever give me any more work."

As I walked around the desk to my chair, I said, "How about *Lesbo Laundromat?*"

"*Lesbo Laundromat?*"

"It's where all these lesbians go to wash their clothes."

"See, McCain," Kenny Thibodeau said patiently, "this stuff isn't as easy as it looks."

"I guess not."

"Are you by any chance a frustrated writer, McCain?"

"Yeah. Sort of, anyway."

"I thought so." Then, quickly: "Not to change the subject but I have some info for you."

"Info?"

Even on a boiling day like today Kenny was decked out in black. He wasn't in mourning. He was just honoring his place in the ranks of the Beat Generation. "I told you I'd play detective and I did. I'm going to write this private-eye novel." Then: "Guess who was caught breaking into Courtney's rectory last night?"

"Who?"

"Dierdre Hall."

"How'd you find that out?"

"I have my ways."

"C'mon, Kenny, how'd you find out?"

"My aunt is their cleaning woman."

"Ah."

"She stopped by my mom's place and I was there."

"Cliffie know this?"

He shook his head. "I don't think. He didn't know as of earlier this morning, anyway."

"Why do you say that?"

"Because my aunt hadn't told him yet."

"Why?"

"She doesn't like Cliffie. She goes to the Lutheran church and he stopped them from playing Bingo one day."

"Didn't Mrs. Courtney turn her in?"

"Mrs. Courtney doesn't know."

"Wasn't she home last night?"

"Oh, she was home, all right. With her bottle. Aunt Am was in the basement. Courtney's lawyer had asked her to start taking an inventory of everything that belonged to the church and everything that belonged to the Courtneys. Mrs. Courtney says she plans to move back east very soon."

"What'd your aunt do with Dierdre?"

"Just told her to go back home. She said the kid was pretty bad off. Crying and stuff."

"She didn't say why she was breaking in?"

"Just said she was looking for something. But wouldn't say what."

A sad, not-unfamiliar scenario was starting to take shape. B-movie, maybe. Or one of Kenny's paperbacks.

"You told anybody this?"

"Only you, counselor. I'm working for you, remember. I figure it's a trade-off."

"Oh?"

"I'll need to ask you a lot of questions about law while I'm writing. I try to make my books as authentic as possible."

"Authentic? I thought you'd never met a lesbian?"

"Well, authentic except for the lesbian parts, I guess."

"But aren't most of the parts about lesbian stuff?"

"What are you, a critic? You want me to keep working or not?"

"You're right, Kenny. Sorry. And this is very useful information. Thanks." Then I said, *"Lost Lesbians."*

"Lost? Where're they lost?"

"Africa? Some desert somewhere?"

"It just doesn't ring right, McCain. Sorry."

"Lesbian Locksmiths?"

He shook his head in pity. "Sorry, McCain."

THERE WAS NO answer at the Halls'. I tried front and back doors, I peeked in windows. I checked backyard, garage, nearby alley.

Why would Dierdre have broken into the rectory last night? Looking for what, exactly?

KENNY THIBODEAU'S AUNT was a nice-looking sixty-year-old woman who lived in a friendly-looking little white house on a nice shady corner of a dead-end street. She was on her haunches gardening when I pulled up. Her graying hair was pulled back into a ponytail and her white U of Iowa T-shirt and jean cut-offs made her seem much younger than she was. Her son had gotten into some speeding trouble several times during the past few years and I'd represented him in court. She greeted me with a raised trowel. "Morning, McCain."

"Morning, Am."

"Plug your ears."

"My ears?"

"These old bones make a lot of noise when I have to stand up."

"You're a doll and you know it."

"I used to be a doll. A long, long time ago I was a doll. Here we go."

Her bones did sort of crackle arthritically.

She wiped the back of a hand across her forehead. "I bet Kenny told you about Dierdre."

"Yeah."

"If you want to know what she was looking for, I don't know."

"You've seen her there before?"

"Oh, sure. She was one of the Reverend's regulars."

"Regulars?"

"He counseled people. I know you didn't care for him but he did a lot of good. I mean, he was sort of stuck-up and a snob and everything. But he saved half a dozen marriages I know of and he got four or five men to quit drinking. Got them into AA."

Every time you try to hate somebody, they go and do something honorable. The inconsiderate bastards.

"And he counseled young people, too, huh?"

"Five or six of them on a regular basis. The Beaumont boy? All the trouble he used to get in? He's been walking the straight and narrow for the past eleven months. Every time I see his mom, she breaks into tears over the Reverend. Says he walks on water and can do no wrong."

"You ever hear any scuttlebutt about his counseling sessions?"

"What kind of scuttlebutt?"

She was about to answer when the mailman appeared in his pith helmet and blue uniform walking shorts and shirt. "There's a nice cold glass of lemonade in the refrigerator for you, Deke. I guess you know where to find it."

"Thanks, Am," Deke said. "You're a lifesaver. As usual." He nodded and left.

"They've got a lot tougher job than most people think. When my husband got laid off at the plant back in '53, he started being a substitute carrier. You never saw so much leg trouble and back trouble and arm trouble. It looks a lot easier than it is. So when it gets real hot, I leave lemonade for Deke in the fridge. He just goes inside and gets it. Even if I'm not here. And I have hot cocoa for him in the winter months."

"You're the one who walks on water."

"Oh, yes," she laughed. "I'm one holy person. That's why Fred and I sit up in bed some nights reading *Playboy* and giggling over the cartoons."

Deke had just set a record for lemonade-guzzling. He was back outside, waving good-bye, going on to the next house.

"What were we talking about?" she said. "Oh, yes, scuttlebutt. No, not really."

"Anybody ever get mad at him about his counseling?"

"A couple of husbands who thought he was taking their wives' side." She smiled. "You know how men are, McCain. You have the misfortune of being one yourself. Here they were happily running around on their wives, and getting stinko in the process, and they deeply resented this minister telling them that *they* were at fault for their unhappy marriages. Why, the nerve of that man!"

"Were they mad enough to kill him?"

"Of the two I'm thinking of, one got a divorce and moved up to the Twin Cities. And the other one finally saw the error of his ways. He's one of the ones who went to AA. And he still goes, too. Things've worked out pretty well for him, in fact."

"You ever hear any scuttlebutt about Dierdre Hall?"

"Well, I don't know if this is scuttlebutt or not but there was a pretty angry argument there one night."

"Between Dierdre and the Reverend?"

"No. Between Sara and the Reverend."

"What happened?"

The phone rang. "Wouldn't you know? I'll be right back, McCain."

She went inside. I watched butterflies, bees, horseflies, robins, dogs, cats...that parade of beings we share the planet with even though we've convinced ourselves that we're the only ones who matter to the history of this nowhere little world.

She came back bearing lemonade. Handed it over.

"Boy, this is good," I said.

She was the picture of the perfect housewife. Except her lemonade was so sour I felt my cheeks puckering inward and my sinus passages starting to drain. No wonder Deke had made it out of there so fast. He knew what was waiting for him. He poured it out in the sink and fled.

"Homemade," she said.

"Mmmm," I said.

"Extra lemons and no sugar," she said.

"Mmmm," I said.

But intrepid detective that I am, I carried on with my questions. "You were telling me about the argument between the Reverend and Sara."

"Oh, right. Well, she just burst in the rectory door one night and ran down the hall and burst into the study where he has his counseling sessions. And started screaming at the Reverend."

"Was Mrs. Courtney home at the time?"

"No. She was out somewhere. She's in a lot of clubs and groups. You know how it is for a minister's wife like that."

"So what happened inside?"

"Well, the first thing Sara did was to send Dierdre home."

"Did Dierdre want to go?"

"No. She was yelling at her mother pretty loudly."

"Could you figure out what they were arguing about?"

"Not really. The Reverend got very angry and told them to keep their voices down. He knew I was somewhere in the house."

"Did Dierdre leave?"

"Uh-huh. She slammed the front door very hard."

"How long did Sara stay?"

"Probably another twenty minutes."

Her phone rang again.

"You're a popular lady."

"Oh, yes, I'm thinking of running for president next time."

"I'd vote for you."

She glanced at my glass. "You hardly touched your lemonade."

"Oh. Sorry. I'll finish it now."

"I'll get the phone."

"I need to leave, anyway. Thanks for talking."

"My pleasure, McCain."

I made sure she didn't see me dump the glass on the far side of the front porch. I set it on the steps and walked to my car.

YOU ALWAYS THINK of burglary as a nighttime occupation.

But I didn't want to wait for night. Things were starting to come clear to me, at least as far as the relationship between Dierdre and Reverend Courtney were concerned. I wondered what Dierdre must have been looking for when she broke in. I also wondered what else there was to learn about Courtney. The most promising place to look was his office in the rectory.

Church and rectory were built into the side of a piney hill. A tranquil, natural setting. Anybody who pulled up in a car could be seen, however, from the street that fronted it.

The first thing to do was to walk up to the front door and ring the bell and see if anybody was inside. I rang. Chimes echoed inside. No response. I knocked. A tabby cat with one injured eye viewed me skeptically from his perch on a low-hanging branch. No response.

I checked the adjacent garage. Empty.

I drove up on top of the hill. A small grocery store sat there. One of the few left, now that the supermarket chains had discovered our little burg. I parked way over on the edge of the gravel drive so the store folks couldn't see me, went inside and bought a pack of Luckies and a pack of Black Jack gum, and then went back outdoors.

Three pairs of tandem-bike riders went past. I figured them all to be about twelve or thirteen. They were at that group-dating stage when you got to hide the crush you had on a girl by going out with a mixed assortment of equally terrified boys and girls. They went inside the store and got soda pop, the girls much more in control of themselves and the situation than the boys, the boys all seeming younger and more callow than the girls in fact, and then they were on their tandem bikes again and rolling down the hill.

Nobody in the parking lot. Nobody driving by to see me.

I started my hike down the hill. The great thing about pine is the smell. The bad thing about pine is the way it stabs you. There was a vague path that wove its way down to the valley. The trees were thick enough here to cool the temperature by several degrees. I used to play Indian in places like these. I always wanted to be the Indian, never the cowboy, never the cavalry. Indians, at least in movies made by white guys, always knew neat stuff, all about caves and how to track mountain lions and how to communicate with smoke signals and pieces of stone smoothed to shine like mirrors. Who wouldn't want to be an Indian?

I was sweaty, piney as a porcupine, and irritable by

the time I reached the backyard of the church. At least the grass had been mowed recently and smelled good.

I had my trusty burglary picks with me—taken in trade from a thief I'd managed to keep out of prison—and a good thing, too. This place was locked up tighter than Jimmy Hoffa's secret bank records. It took me longer to get inside than I'd hoped, thus increasing my chances of being seen. A raccoon sat at the tree line observing me with the kind of wry look only raccoons, of all God's animals, can summon. He seemed to be under the completely mistaken impression that I was some kind of idiot.

Air-conditioning. I just stood in it and let it cool me, balm me, dry me. All I needed was a glass of Aunt Am's lemonade.

Courtney had a lot of the Great Books on his shelves. I suspected he'd actually read them. His den was English manor house with fireplace, leather wing-back chairs, antiques, and a really first-rate collection of smoking pipes. Not a corncob among them.

Since Cliffie had no doubt searched this office, I felt sure that it was worth searching again. Cliffie could overlook a corpse sprawled across a desk.

I spent a good twenty minutes looking. I went through the desk; I went through the books, making sure they weren't false fronts hiding a safe or slot behind them; I got down on my hands and knees and made sure the floor was flat, no trap doors, no insets, no safes.

As I was getting up, I realized that I hadn't checked the in-out tray on his desk. An oversight worthy of Cliffie. I had some luck.

There were four envelopes hand-addressed in a forceful male script. Blue ink. I read them. Letters from

Courtney thanking various members of his flock for favors they'd done the church.

There was a letter folded in half, too. I opened it. It wasn't a letter, though. It was a crude layout for a leaflet.

WHY THE JEWS FAVOR KENNEDY

It was the same creed as always. The Jews wanted to be on the Supreme Court so they could outlaw all the good Christian principles this country was founded on—including letting colored people marry white people (i.e., big black hands soiling virginal white female flesh)—and Kennedy would happily appoint Jews because they would see to it that he was able to serve not just two terms but three or four. The way FDR did.

There was something else folded into the flyer. A check written on the personal account of Reverend Courtney and made out personally to Parnell, the printer. No businesses were named. Looked completely and unsuspiciously like a personal transaction.

"He wasn't very fond of either Jews or Catholics," she said from the doorway. "But then we all have our little failings, don't we, Mr. McCain?"

She would have made a good cover model for *Manhunt* detective magazine just then, a fashionably dressed widow holding a silver-plated .45 in a black-gloved hand, a veil covering the cold, attractive face. A Raymond Chandler wet dream.

The laugh was pained. "When you came right down to it, he wasn't all that crazy about Protestants, either. But he came from five generations of ministers, so he bowed to family pressure and went to divinity school."

"He really believes all that stuff about Jews secretly running the world?"

This time the laugh was bitter. "His one true love—the girl he fell in love with his freshmen year in college—fell in love with a Jewish graduate student. He hated Jews ever since."

"You hate a whole group of people because of one guy? Sounds like he had a few mental problems."

"More than a few—and that's probably why he was such a good counselor, which he was. He could identify with the people he helped. He genuinely cared about them."

"Enough to get one of them pregnant," I said.

I wanted the satisfaction of seeing what was going on behind the veil. All I could hear in response was a tiny, harsh breath. "Did Sara Hall tell you?"

"No. I just put a few stray pieces of information together. Dierdre broke in here looking for something."

"It would've destroyed him. He started to come undone the last six months—ever since he started sleeping with her. And then when she got pregnant—anyway, she'd written him some very foolish letters. That's why she broke in here. She wanted them back."

"And you started drinking again."

I said it without judgment. Merely a statement.

"Yes."

"I'm sorry."

"Believe it or not, I still loved him. He had a difficult life. Spiritually, I mean. Good and evil. It was a constant struggle. He never learned to forgive himself."

It's always instructive to hear somebody else talk about a person you don't like much. How could you both have the same person in mind? A minister who would take advantage of a teenage girl? A man of God who would pay for hate mail and condemn an entire group of people because he lost a girl? How could this possibly be the same man she was describing in terms of a John Donne-ish torment with his demons?

But you know something, it was quite likely that both portraits were true. We're heroes or villains depending on who's talking.

"He had one thing, anyway."

"What's that?"

"A good wife," I said.

The bitter laugh again. "Oh, yes. Such a good wife that I passed out at a dinner party the night the dean of the divinity school gave a party for his best students. And one time—at his first church assignment—I tripped and fell walking down the aisle to the front of the church. Dead drunk. And a lot of traffic accidents, Mr. McCain. Thank the Lord I didn't hurt anybody. I wake up in cold sweats sometimes, thinking I've run over a child—" She was crying now.

I went over and took the gun from her. No bravery on my part. It was pointed at the floor by now anyway. I slipped it into my trouser pocket. She came against me in a rustle of black organdy. She slid her arms around my neck. I eased her hat and veil away and let her weep.

When I felt my groin starting to react automatically to the pressure of her body against mine, I helped her across the floor and eased her down on the couch. I took her pumps off and got a pillow behind her head. There was a bottle of spring water on a small sidebar.

I poured a glass and held it to her lips. She drank. "Thank you."

I went over and sat down in one of the leather wing chairs and lit a Lucky.

"I need to ask you some questions."

"I'll try to answer them."

"What was he doing out at Muldaur's church the night Muldaur died?"

"Muldaur was blackmailing him."

"What? Are you sure?"

She nodded. Put the back of a hand to her head. "In my purse outside the door there are some aspirin. I have a terrible headache. Could you get me those, please?"

I got them, lifted her head the way I would have a sick person's, and put the aspirin on her tongue.

"You're giving me communion, Mr. McCain." She smiled. She was a good-looking woman.

"I guess I missed my calling."

I went over, rescued my cigarette from the ashtray, and sat down again.

"What did Muldaur have on him?"

"The way I understand it—and this may not be exactly correct—is that Muldaur and one of his friends were out hunting for snakes one afternoon. There's a small fishing cabin near where they were. The cabin was owned by an old man who belonged to our church. When he passed on, the widow insisted that Thomas take the key to the cabin and use it whenever he liked. He took Dierdre out there several times—he'd gotten very stupid about her, he told me; he said he hadn't felt lust like this in years—" The smile again, sweet, self-deprecating. "Which isn't exactly what a wife wants to hear."

"I don't imagine."

"But I didn't blame him. All the hell I'd put him

through with my drinking—we'd quit being lovers a long time ago. Or he had anyway. I was more like his sister or his daughter than his wife—at least as he saw it—somebody he was obligated to take care of. That's not uncommon among alcoholic spouses. They stick by the alcoholic but the romance goes and rarely ever comes back.''

''I'm sorry,'' I said. Then, ''Could you please tell me a little more about Muldaur?''

''Well, he was a piece of work, wasn't he? The snakes. And blackmailing people. And sleeping with women in his own congregation.'' She caught herself. ''I guess except for the snakes, I could be describing my husband, couldn't I? That never occurred to me before just now. That my husband and Muldaur were similar in that respect. They were both men of the cloth who'd seriously violated their vows. If Muldaur ever took any vows.''

''Why did your husband have Sara Hall with him that night at Muldaur's?''

''They were going to talk to Muldaur. We aren't wealthy. Muldaur was getting $500 a month from my husband and it was breaking us. That's about what he makes for a monthly income. All our clothes and his fancy cars...they came from a trust fund I inherited. But that's about gone now. He'd raided our pathetic little savings account to pay Muldaur as it was.''

''What about the sportscar?''

She rolled over on her side, watching me. ''Do you suppose I could have a cigarette?''

''Sure.''

I got a fresh one going the way Robert Ryan would have and carried it, along with an ashtray, over to her. She sat up on an elbow, inhaled deeply.

"He didn't want me to smoke."

"It's not good for you."

"Yes, I notice *you* don't smoke."

"I'm down to three cartons a day."

"I'm surprised."

"About what?"

"You. I sort of like you. And all the time I thought you were just this grubby little creep that worked for Judge Whitney."

"I have that right on my business card. Grubby little creep. At your service."

Another deep inhalation. "What were we talking about?"

"About how your husband could afford a sports-car."

"A gift from the last church."

"Ah."

"They didn't find out until after we'd left that he'd been seeing three or four of the choir women on the side."

"I see a pattern here."

"Oh, it was definitely a pattern. Same as my drinking was—is—a pattern. Life is patterns, Mr. McCain."

"Yeah, I've kinda noticed that." Then: "You never did tell me what Sara Hall and your husband were doing at Muldaur's church the night he was killed."

"They were going to beg him to stop blackmailing my husband. We were running out of money and she was afraid Muldaur would tell somebody about my husband and Dierdre. And then eventually the whole town would know she was pregnant."

"They really thought Muldaur would back off?"

"Last-ditch effort." A long trail of smoke. "As I

said, we didn't have much money left. And Sara was terrified of what Muldaur would do.''

''You know a guy named Bill Oates?''

''No. Why?''

''I saw him arguing with his wife the night Muldaur died. And then I saw him in Muldaur's trailer very early in the morning later on. Made me curious about his relationship with Viola Muldaur.''

''You think he might have killed Muldaur?''

''He looks like a possibility.''

''Anybody else?''

''You.''

''Are you kidding?''

She sat up. The leather sofa made a lot of noise.

''Afraid not.''

''Why would I kill my husband?''

''Isn't it obvious?''

''And did I also kill Muldaur?''

''Probably. But that's the trouble I'm having with all this.''

''Do you ever read Nero Wolfe?''

''All the time.''

''You know how he always makes those astonishing leaps of deductive logic?''

''I wish I knew how he did it. The question is—who would have a motive to kill both your husband and Muldaur?''

''Are you saying that you've eliminated me?''

''Not necessarily.''

''But why would I have killed Muldaur?''

''Look at the time sequence. Maybe you were so sick of Muldaur blackmailing your husband that you killed him with that poison.''

''That makes sense I suppose—may I mooch another cig, by the way?—but if I killed Muldaur why would I turn around and kill my husband?''

I brought her another cigarette. She lit it from the butt of the one she was finishing.

When I was seated again, I said, ''You kill Muldaur. Everything looks good for a day or so. And then your husband tells you he wants a divorce. Or you find that he's sleeping with another one of the choir ladies again. You could have a lot of motives. Especially if you were on the bottle again. Alcoholics aren't very rational when they're tipping a few.''

''Very neat. Nero would be proud of you.''

She sure did enjoy cigarettes. She smoked with great erotic enthusiasm. My groin was starting to make itself felt again.

''The only thing wrong with it is that it isn't true, Mr. McCain.''

''So say you.''

''So say I.''

I stood up. Stubbed my Lucky out. Walked to the door. ''I need to go.''

''I could always tell Cliffie you broke into my house.''

''I could always tell Cliffie your husband was a blackmailer.''

She smiled. ''I guess that's a good point.'' Then: ''I'm curious.''

''What?''

''A minute or so ago—were you looking at me— sexually?''

''Boy, what a question.''

''Well, were you?''

''Yeah, I guess I was.''

''Thank you. Thank you very much. It's been such

a long time since I felt a young man's eyes on me that way. The proper alcoholic wife of a minister doesn't get a lot of looks like that. I lost fifteen years when I saw your eyes settle on my breasts and legs.'' Tears touched her eyes and voice. ''It felt so good.''

''My pleasure,'' I said. ''You're a very good-looking woman.''

A teary laugh.

I thought of going over there to give her a reassuring hug. But given the moment, that was probably a very risky move.

I said good-bye and left.

THERE WERE TWO people I wanted to talk to. Reluctant as I was to go back to Muldaur's place—my ankle, since you've probably been worrying about it, the considerate people you are—hurt only at certain angles. I just wasn't sure which angles those were. So I'd be moving along just fine and then I'd step down just so and—one of life's little mysterious games.

The top of Muldaur's shabby trailer had been painted silver and shone like a mirror in the stabbing rays of the sun. I decided not to take any chances with men with shotguns bursting out the door. I brought my own .45, which was the gun my dad carried in the war.

I knocked several times. No answer. No dog bark. No human voice. No radio blare. No TV drone. I took this to mean, in my worldly way, that probably nobody was home or that if somebody was home, he or she didn't plan to come out.

Then I heard the singing. Sweet and high and mountain-stream pure, no affectation, no straining for effect, a simple, sincere young girl's voice singing one of those old hillbilly hymns you could catch on ''Grand

Ole Opry'' or ''Country Jubilee'' every once in a while.

My assumption at first was that it was a record or a radio. But as I turned I realized that it was coming from the church. I let it pull me, eager to hear it more clearly, and moments later I stood in the cooling shadows of the old service garage, listening to Ella Muldaur sing.

Ella stood in the center of the platform, a radiant hill child in a tattered blouse and faded jeans. Viola sat in the chair next to her, dressed in a pair of overalls and a blouse.

''Oh, I have talked to Jesus,
And He said He will show me peace.
Oh, I have talked to Jesus,
And He promised me no more grief.''

Her voice was skilled and knowing enough to convey both the promised peace and the grief of the present time. No wonder Viola was crying, as she had been that first night I'd seen them here on the altar.

She held Ella's right hand as the girl sang and swayed in joy and sorrow to the melody. And for that moment I was able to put aside all the hip, modern ways I'd been taught to feel about our quest for purpose and meaning and to simply share in our need to understand our place in the cosmos. Cave paintings dating back thousands of years illustrated the desperate need mankind had always felt in seeking such an explanation. It almost didn't matter if you believed in a god-force or not. The need to bring some meaning to the spectacle of human history was primal.

And so gentle and soothing when put into song by this girl.

They were so caught up in Ella's singing they didn't even seem aware of me at first.

And then she was done. And I felt banished from celestial comfort. I was no longer elevated by my humanity but doomed to it. It was not in heaven I stood but in an old garage that smelled of car oil and filth.

"You shouldn't be here," Viola said.

"I'm here to see Ella."

"Ella? What for?"

I was only halfway up the aisle. I stood in place.

"The other day she said she had something to tell me. I'm curious what that was going to be."

"I shouldn't't've said that, mister," Ella said.

"That's the most beautiful singing I've ever heard."

"You should not praise the Lord's music," Viola snapped. "Only the Devil wants worldly praise. Ella sings beautiful because her soul is beautiful. Ella is the purest of us all. She is God's favored child."

"Ella's old enough to speak for herself," I said.

"Please, mister, you're gonna get me in an awful lot of trouble. And besides, all I was gonna say was that my daddy, he got sick even before he came to the altar that night."

"You hush, girl!" Viola said. "We don't talk to this man."

"Yes, Mama!"

"Now, you leave, McCain. Or I'll have Bill Oates spend some more time with you." She grinned. "He told me how he done you pretty mean the other night."

"You don't seem very interested in finding the man who killed your husband, Mrs. Muldaur."

"All I'm interested in is you gettin' out of my sight."

Not much I could say to that.

FIFTEEN

BILL OATES LIVED ON an acreage on the north side of
the town. A hundred yards or so from his dirt driveway
was the "City Limits" sign. He'd planted half an acre
of corn and some soybeans and there were a few head
of cattle on a wide patch of grazing land. People who
couldn't make a living farming anymore often lived on
places like this. They worked in town but kept a hand
in the farm life they'd grown up with.

The outbuildings—good-size barn and a large wooden
shed, maybe for chickens—were in decent shape and the
John Deere tractor parked near the back of the house
looked to be in fine repair, too.

The inevitable farm collie rushed at me in the inevitable way and made all the inevitable noises and
threats until a tired-looking woman even more faded
than her housedress shushed him and shooed him and
then came out, screen door snapping shut behind her,
to meet me. She'd apparently been baking. Her hands
were white with flour.

"Help you?"

"My name's McCain."

"I know who you are." Not at all friendly.

Wide face, smart but angry blue eyes, reddish hair
just starting to go gray. And a very nice body if you
liked them voluptuous, body that performed all the

functions of eating, sleeping, working but that she probably never gave much thought to otherwise. Mid-thirties, most likely.

"The mister ain't home."

"Then I'd like to talk to you."

She held up her hands for inspection. "I'm baking pies."

I knew I had only a few seconds left before she ordered me back to my car. "I was out at Muldaur's church the night he died."

"Yeah, I seen you. So did everybody else."

"Muldaur asked me to be there."

"Muldaur's dead, like you say."

"Your husband slapped you that night."

"How'd you find that out?"

"I saw it."

"Oh."

"I'd like you to tell me why he slapped you."

"That wouldn't be any of your business, mister. And anyways, I thought Sykes was the law in these parts."

I grinned. "More or less."

"You ain't even half as cute as you think you are."

"I'll try to remember that." I didn't have anything to lose so I said, "Were you friendly with Muldaur?"

She spat into the dust. "You got a lot of nerve askin' a Christian woman a question like that."

"Two men have been murdered. I need to know why."

"Somebody tell you something about me?" More suspicious now than angry.

"No. But I'm learning things about Reverend Muldaur. And I just thought it was strange that your husband would hit you like that."

"He hits me all the time like that. I need to be hit all the time like that."

I thought of what Parnell had told me about how a good church should make you feel bad. My God is a wrathful God.

"Any particular reason?"

"There was a time in my life when I wandered."

"Wandered?"

She looked over at the collie. The dog had a long, sweet face. She looked as if she sympathized with the woman's wandering.

"I used to wander off with other men."

"I see."

"I had the Devil in me."

"That's why he slapped you?"

"Used to be why he slapped me. Then we moved up here from Georgia and the wandering stopped."

"But he kept hitting you?"

She stared at me. "I'm a sinner, mister. I done a lot of other terrible things. I mean, it wasn't just the wanderin'. I don't always keep the house clean the way God wants me to, I don't always fix Bill the meals he wants the way God wants me to, I don't always do the things in our marriage bed God said I should do even though it hurts me when I do them. I'm a coward about pain. I even hated my own children when they was bein' born because I was in so much pain. I'm not a good woman, mister. So Bill's got every right in the world to hit me."

"He found out about you and Muldaur?"

She spat in the dust. "Git. And git now."

"I'll find out eventually, Mrs. Oates. If not from you, somebody you know. Things like this get around."

Hard-eyed, hard-voiced, she said, "You must think you're pretty big stuff. Goin' around and judgin' people like this."

"I'm not judging you, Mrs. Oates. I'm a sinner just like you. No better, no worse."

That seemed to affect her. She touched a flour-white hand to her hair, as if for the first time she was concerned about her appearance. As if for the first time, she saw me as human and thus somebody to look presentable for.

She shrugged. "He found out a week before John died. He had his suspicions and he just kept workin' on me."

"What did he do?"

"He sent the girls to stay down to his in-laws and then he tied me up in our bedroom. Tied me up naked and then he beat me with his razor strop. Beat me on my body so nobody could see it. He didn't want nobody to know what I'd done and I didn't blame him. I'd wandered again and I had promised him on God's holy head that I wouldn't. I'd even been able to handle the snakes a few times without them biting me. Now, after what I done with John, they'd kill me sure. They're demons, you know."

Then: "So he let me go after a few days. He carried on, though, even after he let me go."

"Carried on?"

"Cried and pounded his fists against the walls and got so drunk he kept falling down. I could see what I done to this man and I wanted to take my life and that's God's truth, mister. I wanted to take my life. But I'd be damned to hell if I did and I knew it, what with my two young ones and all. Who'd take care of them?

That's the first thing God would ask me. Who's gonna take care of your girls now, Pam?"

I heard the panel truck before I saw it. It rattled like a wagonload of pots and pans. It came up the driveway about forty miles an hour, lost in its own dust.

We both watched as he jumped out of the car. Oates. He had a shotgun in his arm. Pointed at me.

He said nothing. Just charged at me.

"Bill!" Pam Oates cried.

But it was too late. He swung the rifle barrel toward the side of my head, the same thing he'd done to me in the empty church.

But for reasons of manliness I suppose—I'd seen an awful lot of Roy Rogers movies growing up—I decided I was too pissed to care at this point. He had pushed me, shoved me, pounded me long enough.

I ducked under the barrel of his weapon. My foot caught him directly in the crotch.

I jumped to his left, while he was still trying to absorb his pain, and slammed a fist into the side of his head. The crotch kick had forced him to stoop so reaching his face was no longer a problem. I doubled up and put a fist against his nose, too. Blood sprayed out of his left nostril. I can't speak for him but I was having a hell of a good time.

Pam took the opportunity to yank the rifle from his hands.

"Now, get in the house, Bill. And I'm afraid you'll have to leave now, McCain. And I don't want to see you back anytime soon. You understand what I'm sayin'?"

"Yes, ma'am."

"Because the next time, I'm callin' Sykes."

Her husband, in pain and shame, had already reached the back door and was going inside.

The violence had disoriented the collie and I felt sorry for her. She was running around in frantic circles, obviously not comprehending the exact nature of what was going on here but very affected—dismayed, startled—by the air of violence. A hot, sleepy day on the acreage was not supposed to be like this.

Pam Oates followed me back to the car.

"He's a good man."

"I'll take your word for it."

"He's never wandered off on me."

I wondered about his wandering and why he'd been at Muldaur's trailer with Viola so early. Maybe he wasn't quite as innocent as Pam thought. He was likely the man who'd fired at Muldaur. Sleeping with a man's wife can get you in that sort of trouble sometimes. But this wasn't exactly the time to raise the question.

She touched my car with an almost shocking tenderness. Her touch had a sexual quality to it. "Boy from Macon used to drive up and see me—this was before I knew John—and he had a nice convertible, too. We had some fun in that car." Her face and voice lost twenty years. "We sure did have some fun."

I ATE A late lunch at the Rexall counter. Lunch-dinner, I guess. I probably wouldn't be eating much more today. Between the heat and my frustration with the case, I was ready to lie on the floor in front of the fan and the TV and be entertained.

Rexall was pretty busy. Bug spray, suntan lotion, charcoal starter, charcoal briquettes, cigarettes, and beer seemed to be the most popular items at the cash register. The air-conditioning was freezing but that was all right after the baking sun.

I looked over the men's adventure magazines. I never bought them but I sure had a good time looking at the covers of he-men fighting off Nazis, Nazi alligators, Nazi snakes, Nazi bats (rabid, of course). The cover quotes were what I enjoyed most of all. And this month's batch had some honeys. "Sexual Psychopaths...Oversexed Women!" "Nympho Outlaw and Her Legion of Outcasts!" "Nazis Dive-Bombed My Body!" "Confessions of a Nazi Call Girl!" My favorite was "Nude Queen of the Communist Cannibals!" Whoever came up with the commie cannibals deserved a bonus. Now that was real writing.

Kylie was at the checkstand. Looking sweet but nervous, she set a small boxcar load of cosmetics on the counter.

"You don't wear all this stuff."

"I thought I'd really get dolled up tonight."

"You don't need dolling up, kiddo. You're a good-looking girl."

"You're prejudiced, McCain. You like me."

"He's your husband. I'm assuming he likes you, too."

She bit her lower lip, half-whispered, "You should see what I'm up against, McCain. She looks like a movie starlet."

I wanted to hold her, protect her. Any man who could throw away a young woman this bright, this decent, this caring—but she had to go through with this, I knew. Same as I'd had to go through it with Pamela Forrest all those years. Being desperately in love is grand, isn't it?

She nodded to my ham and cheese. "You should eat better."

"I know. Usually, Mrs. Goldman fixes me meals three or four times a week. But her sister took sick all of a sudden."

"Where's her sister?"

"Des Moines."

I saw how her right hand was twitching. It made her even more vulnerable.

"I wish I was in Des Moines, McCain."

"You'll be fine."

"I try to be objective about it, you know."

"One thing you can't be objective about is being in love with somebody."

"I mean, I really can't blame him."

"I can."

"I'm what you'd call pretty, I guess."

"Very pretty."

"But you should see her, McCain. She makes me want to hide in the basement."

"Is she as smart as you are? As much fun as you are? As deep as you are?"

"Oh, McCain, I'm not deep."

"Are you kidding? You know things, Kylie. You understand things. You have insight into people."

"I don't fill out a bikini very well."

"I happen to've seen you in a bikini one time. And you filled it out just right."

"And my nose— You know, back east a lot of Jewish girls get bobs."

"You don't need a Bob. Or a Dave. Or a Rick."

She smiled.

"You've got a very fine nose. It fits your face perfectly."

We went through this every once in a while. Her insecurities ran pretty wide. But then again, so did mine. I figured that's why we liked each other.

"You'll be fine tonight. You just have to relax."

"It's like a first date. And look how long we've been married."

I held her hand. "You'll do fine."

"Really?"

"Really."

She asked about the case and I told her what I'd learned. She tried to seem interested but her anxiety made that impossible. She said good-bye and fled.

I HATE TO admit this but that night I drank more than my usual two beers. I drank three beers. Which meant, given my size and my inability to hold alcohol at all well, I was pretty stinko.

I banged my knee going to the bathroom, I banged my head getting a slice of cold pizza from the refrigerator, and I banged my butt when I miscalculated how far the end of the coffee table extended.

My dad and I are about the world's worst drinkers. It takes most accomplished drinkers a long time to get stupid when they drink. We can do it in about the length of time it takes to guzzle a beer-and-a-half.

Things get all out of proportion for us. Something mildly amusing becomes unbearably hilarious. Something modestly sad becomes a cause for great theatrical tears.

Tonight, for instance, Art Carney did a routine on "The Honeymooners" that made me laugh so hard I had to dash (well, stumble forward quickly) to the bathroom before I yellowed my Sears underwear; and then on "Gunsmoke" they had this story about a young crippled girl who becomes a gunfighter in order to avenge her brother, and man, tears were dripping off my chin when she got killed in the end.

I had the great good sense to go to bed shortly after that.

Sometimes in the sticky murk of sleep—not even the fan cooled things off in any substantial way—the phone rang. Rang several times. Rang loud enough to stir me but not loud enough to make me pick it up.

I fell back to sleep.

The phone started ringing again and this time, I picked it up.

"Hullo."

"McCain?"

"Uh-huh."

"Have you been drinking?"

"Never."

"This is Judge Whitney."

"Yes, I recognized you. You're sort of hard to confuse with anybody else."

"Get some coffee in you and then head for the jail. I'll meet you there."

"The jail? What for?"

"Cliffie, Jr., in his infinite wisdom, has just arrested Sara Hall for murdering Muldaur and Courtney."

PART III

SIXTEEN

YOU HAVE TO WONDER how word could spread at three o'clock in the morning. No air-raid sirens had sounded, no words were bellowed from the loudspeakers the city had planted in various places, no Paul Revere had hopped in his car and driven up and down the dark streets announcing that Sara Hall had been arrested for murder.

And yet there they were, maybe as many as fifteen of them, looking like the kind of crowd you always saw in westerns, the low-murmuring crowd that could turn into a lynch mob when the guy in the black hat appeared and stirred them up.

Except people in those westerns didn't wear pink hair curlers that made them look like Martians, or Cubs baseball caps and Monkey Ward sleeveless undershirts that emphasized hairy, beachball-like stomachs. And in westerns Annette Funicello wasn't playing on car radios.

Main Street was empty otherwise, and shadowy, and like the people in the crowd, it suggested a movie, too, small-town Americana. I glimpsed a shooting star and then heard the steady sound of a plane lost in the clouds. Any kind of plane sound suggested only one thing to Americans these days. That's why we taught civil defense in our schools—''Duck and cover''—and that's why forty percent of us, according to the Eastern newspapers, were busy building some form of bomb shelter. There were a lot of jokes going around about what Hugh Hefner would put in his bomb shelter.

One of Cliffie's cousins—a dense deputy named Jebby Sykes—stood in front of the front door of the jail with a shotgun in his arms. He didn't look scared. He looked sleepy and he looked rumpled.

"Hey, where you goin', McCain?"

"Little pecker, he thinks he's hot stuff, don't he?"

"Him and that damn Judge Whitney!"

I should have known that it would not be the hard-working people of town who would tumble out of bed in the middle of the night to see somebody prominent thrown in jail.

No, it would be Cliffie's vast array of cousins, shirt-tail kin, and mutants who would find this so thrilling. Just imagine, one of them high-tone women who bathed regularly and wore clean clothes spending the night in Uncle Cliffie's jail. Who could ask for a bigger thrill than that?

"You got cause to be here, McCain?"

He got all swole up the way unimportant people do when they're trying to be important, all swole up with his badge and his wrinkled uniform and his Remington shotgun, all swole up keeping the hair-curlers and the Cubbies caps at bay, all swole up because nobody had ever let him be before. And it was almost sad. That was the terrible thing about the Sykes family. But every once in a while their coarseness, vulgarity, greed, ruthlessness, and stupidity made you sad, too. They were, in the cosmic sense, your brothers and sisters. And there wasn't a damned thing you could do about it.

"I'm supposed to meet Judge Whitney here, Jebby."

"She's inside. But that don't mean I got to let you in."

"Are you still mad because I caught your fly ball that day?"

"You damn right I—" Then stopped himself.

"What fly ball he talking about, Jebby?" said a mostly toothless man.

"Never you mind, Cousin Bob," Jebby said. He looked pained. "Cliff said I was to pack you people up in your cars and get you back home. Otherwise he's gonna gnaw on me somethin' terrible. Now, will you do that for me?"

"Maybe she'll try'n escape," somebody said.

"Yeah, and then Cliff would have to shoot her," said another.

"Now, we wouldn't want to miss somethin' like that," said the first.

Jebby scowled.

"She ain't gonna escape. She's really ladylike. How'd she ever get outta jail? No, now you folks get back home before Cliff gets mad at me. Please. I promise to have my mama make you some of her special rhubarb pie for the family reunion this year."

"Enough for everybody, Jebby?"

"Enough for everybody."

A woman said, "You know how Cliff can be on people who work for him. Maybe we better leave Jebby here alone."

"She escapes, though, don't forget them dogs of mine," a man said.

I wanted to ask if anybody had any tanks or B-52s.

Sara Hall was a dangerous woman. You couldn't be too careful.

They all said their good-nights, and now there was something peaceful about them and their shabbiness made me feel guilty for always holding myself to be so superior to people like them, and then they left.

"That was a home run. You stole it."

"I didn't steal it," I said.

"It was over the center field fence."

"Yeah, but I caught it, didn't I?"

He looked at me squarely. He was just faintly cross-eyed.

"That would've been the only homer I ever hit. I wanted my folks to be proud of me. My daddy was at that game. He had that heart condition. I wanted him to see me do good at somethin' because he always said I was like him, that I wasn't good at nothin'. He died about two weeks later."

Ninth grade that had been. Ten years ago. I'd felt so damned good about making the catch, all the way back to the wall in the American Legion baseball park built over by the old swimming pool, all the way back to the wall, snatching it from being a certain home run. God, I'd strutted around. Major leagues, here I come. But knowing all the time that I was just about like Jebby, I wasn't much good at things either, not the manly things so treasured by all boys, not good with hammer, not good with football, not good with car engine, not good with simple physical labor that required even the dimmest skill. And for that wonderful moment—my teammates patting me on the back and telling me what a great player I was—I was good at the manly and thus important things. It had been pure fluke to catch it and now here was Jebby telling me that it had been pure fluke to hit it.

"God, I'm sorry I brought it up, Jebby. I just said it to piss you off."

He shrugged. "I don't blame you, McCain. Neither of us was worth a shit." He smiled. His slightly crossed eyes smiled, too. "It was time for one of us losers to have a little bit of luck, wasn't it? You was never mean to us Sykeses the way some of them was, so if anybody had to catch the homer of mine, I'm glad it was you."

Then he stood back and said, "The Judge, she's in Cliff's office."

THE JUDGE WAS in Cliffie's office, all right. He was crouching in his desk chair, doing everything but covering his face with his arms, while she shouted at him and blew Gauloise smoke in his face. Not even his crisp khaki uniform and all the framed photos of him holding various types of rifles, shotguns, howitzers, could make him look in control of this moment.

"The idea of arresting one of this town's most upstanding citizens—and my best friend—is ridiculous. You know and I know, Cliffie, that this is just one more of your little games to embarrass me as the only intelligent representative of law and order in this town!"

Oh, she was blistering. Oh, she was bombastic. Oh, she was absolutely right. What sort of reason would Cliffie have for arresting poor Sara Hall? And she did all this in a white shirt, dark slacks, and a blue suede car coat that cost a lot more than my ragtop.

"You always have to arrest somebody, don't you,

and it's always the wrong person, isn't it?" she concluded.

Which is what I asked him as soon as the Judge saw me and gave me the floor. "You had to arrest somebody, didn't you, Cliffie? You just can't let a few days pass without throwing somebody in that pigsty of a jail of yours, can you?"

"We clean it once a week. And we clean it good."

"Yeah, but the drunks puke in it every night," I said.

"I don't want to coddle prisoners the way you two do. The smell of puke'll be an incentive to stay out of jail."

The Judge looked at me and said, "He's medieval."

"And moronic."

"And malevolent."

"And malignant."

"And a lot of other M words," she sneered, "if we just had time to go through them all."

With "malevolent" and "malignant" Cliffie's face had gone blank. He was still trying to figure out what they meant.

"I'm holding her on a charge of first-degree murder," he said, sitting up straight, trying to convince us, and himself, that he was back in control.

"You're forgetting something, Cliffie," I said.

"What?"

"She's the judge with jurisdiction in this case." I pointed to the Judge.

"Yeah? Big deal."

"It is a big deal, Cliffie," I said. "She can set bail."

"And I'm setting bail right now," the Judge interjected. "Ten dollars."

"That's crazy! Nobody sets a ten-dollar bail in a murder case."

"I do," Judge Whitney said.

"I'm gonna file a motion," he said.

"What sort of motion?" I said.

"To the state Supreme Court."

Actually, they'd probably not only hear his motion but also agree with him that a ten-dollar bail was ridiculous.

"Do you have a fin on you?" Judge Whitney said. Sometimes, she tries to sound like Barbara Stanwyck.

"I think you mean a sawbuck."

"A sawbuck. Do you have one?"

I nodded and got out my wallet. Have you ever noticed how rich people never seem to carry cash? Could that possibly account for how they got rich in the first place?

I slapped it down on Cliffie's desk.

"I hereby grant this bail," Judge Whitney said. "Now go get Sara."

"You gotta fill out forms."

"You'll have your forms in the morning. Now go get Sara."

"Stash!"

Stash was the night deputy.

"Why'd you arrest her, Cliffie?" I said.

"Don't call me Cliffie or I'll arrest *you*."

"You didn't have anything on her."

"The hell I didn't."

"Oh? Like what?"

"Like a tip to look in her garage. And guess what I found there?"

Stash, a guy with a ducktail haircut that was greasier than Jerry Lee Lewis', peeked in and said, "Uh-huh."

"Stash, go get the Hall broad and bring her here."

He finger-popped Cliffie and said, "Gotcha, Chief."

"The Hall broad," the Judge said under her breath.

"So what did you find?" I asked after Stash and his very loud heel-clips disappeared to the back and the jail.

"I found a can of strychnine just where the caller said it would be."

"Was the caller a man or woman?"

"I don't have to tell you squat."

"Man or woman, Cliffie?"

He grinned. "Well, it was one or the other."

"Moronic," the Judge said.

"No, we used that word already."

"Mediocre, then."

I smiled. "That's almost a compliment for somebody like Cliffie."

Stash and his heel clips were back. A disheveled Sara Hall fell into the arms of her friend the Judge and the Judge, without once looking back at Cliffie or saying good-bye to me, left with Sara in tow. On the other side of the door, Sara glanced back at me and I knew then that she knew I'd broken my word to her and told the Judge about Dierdre's pregnancy. It wasn't a hateful glance, just a weary one. I'd betrayed her and she'd never trust me again. I suppose in the cosmic scheme of things it didn't matter a whole hell of a lot. But I certainly felt ashamed of myself, and sad that she'd never again count me as a friend.

"Ten dollars," Cliffie said. "I can't believe it."

"Hell, Cliffie," I said, watching him again," she could've made it five."

A WEEPING DIERDRE was led into the long dining room ten minutes after we arrived at Judge Whitney's. The

Judge ordered breakfast for everybody and then we all sat down with cigarettes and coffee—the Judge, of course, drinking brandy—to figure out exactly what to do next.

"Was it your rat strychnine he found?" I asked Sara.

"I'd never seen it before."

"Did he present you with a search warrant?"

"Yes."

"Where were you while all this was going on?" I asked Dierdre.

"Being sick," she said. "I'm still sick." She touched her stomach. "The baby."

"Did Cliffie dust for fingerprints?"

"Not that I saw. He came to the front door and pounded and pounded till I woke up. He left his emergency lights on. Which woke up all the neighbors, of course. It was very embarrassing."

"So then he led you out to the garage?"

"Yes. Then he started looking around."

"And he found the poison."

She nodded. Then: "I'm picturing it now. He just picked it up. He couldn't have looked for fingerprints."

"Good old Cliffie."

The staff didn't look all that happy about being awakened in the middle of the night to feed us. I was thinking I'd have to train my inherited cats to cook. Then any time I wanted something to eat—

We ate and didn't talk much while we did so. I had scrambled eggs, toast, orange juice, and more coffee. I felt vaguely entitled to renew my membership in the human race. I still needed a shave and a shower but the food was doing wondrous things for my brain and attitude.

"Did you ever threaten to kill Muldaur?" I said when we got rolling again.

"No."

"Did you ever threaten to kill Courtney?"

"Several times."

"Did anybody hear you?"

"His wife. And probably the housekeeper."

"His wife? Did she say anything to you?"

Sara Hall hesitated. "I'm trying to remember. She'd had to hear us arguing. I heard steps on the floor outside the door. A dead spot in the wood. You know how older houses are. I got the impression she was listening."

"So she may have heard everything you said about Dierdre?"

"Yes."

Even though I'd gone over this with Mrs. Courtney, hearing it from Sara gave it all more emotion. What kind of impact would it have on a woman when she first learned that her husband had gotten a teenage girl pregnant? And him a minister, no less.

"Did you see anybody around your yard lately? Any strange faces?"

"No," she said. "Honey?"

Dierdre was barely hanging on. Any moment now she'd be racing to the john again. "No. But then I wouldn't have noticed, anyway, Mom. I've been too busy puking."

"There's no reason to talk that way at a dinner table," the Judge said.

"She was only kidding, Esme," Sara said.

"Nonetheless."

And Dierdre was off again. To the bathroom.

I was writing some things down in my notebook when Sara said, "I just thought of something."

"What?"

"I was in the backyard taking laundry down from the line—this was right at dusk—when I noticed this truck down the alley."

"What kind of truck?"

She described it.

"It looked familiar for some reason," she said.

"You remember when this was?"

"I'm not sure but I think it was the day after Courtney was killed."

The truck was duly noted in my notebook. It belonged to Muldaur. I decided not to say anything for now.

"You see anybody in it?"

"No."

"Around it?"

"Not that—no, not that I can think of."

"How long was it there?"

"I don't know. I didn't really think anything of it. I just took the wash and went back inside."

There was more. Lots more, in fact. But nothing useful. I had another piece of toast and another cup of coffee; Dierdre got sick again; the staff, eager to get back to sleep so they'd catch at least a few hours of blissful rest, began making an awful lot of noise to convey their displeasure with us. The Judge returned their glares but this time of night, they were willing to stand up to her. They weren't intimidated.

Sara and Dierdre stayed there for the night.

The Judge walked me outside. It was that thrilling time of night, just before dawn as all the mysteries of evening begin to vanish and day, reluctantly, begins to reassert itself.

It was actually chilly and it felt good.

"She didn't do it," the Judge said.

"I know."

"I feel so sorry for her."

"So do I."

"And I'd like to strangle that little idiot Dierdre."

Given the condition my sister had left town in, there wasn't much I could say.

"People do foolish things, Judge. And you and me."

"Nice of you to remind me." She lighted one Gauloise off another, pitched the butt into a hedge. "Get a few hours' sleep and then get back at it, McCain. Dick will be here late tomorrow afternoon. In a few hours, this place will be hell with all the Secret Service men. They'll be stringing phone lines and setting up checkpoints and clearing gawkers out of the way and— but it'll be worth it to see him again. He's a very charming man."

"Yes, I've noticed that."

"I'm being serious, McCain, and you're being sarcastic."

"I guess I'll have to take your word on the charming part. He's about the most wooden politician I've ever seen. He always wears a suit, no matter what. Does the guy ever relax?"

"Ever relax? When he was out here for the caucus last year, you should've seen him playing croquet in my backyard. This year we're going to play volleyball."

"Gosh, I sure hope so. Dick Nixon playing volleyball. How lucky could I get to see that?"

"Get out of here, McCain, before I have Cliffie arrest you."

"On what charge?"

She allowed herself the tiniest of smirks. "For being insufferable, of course. You were born insufferable, McCain, and I'm sorry to say you'll die insufferable."

THE PHONE WOKE me around nine-thirty that morning.

Tasha was sleeping on my chest, where she usually was whenever I slept on my back, Crystal slept near my head, and Tess was at my feet. Biting them.

"Yes?"

"You're still asleep."

"I was till you called. Shouldn't you be writing *Lesbo Landscapers* or something?"

"That's not all that bad, McCain. For just waking up."

"Do I get my National Book Award now or later?"

"Later. After you go see Muldaur's first wife."

"You going to tell me something, Kenny?"

"I told you I'm really getting into this private-eye jazz. It's fun."

"So who's his first wife?"

"Bill Oates' wife, Pam."

"You're kidding. How'd you find that out?"

"Guy down the block works out at the quarry where Oates does."

I eased out of bed, eased a Lucky between my lips, eased a book of paper matches into my right hand. I knew how to strike one with only one hand. Any time I got down on myself for not accomplishing much in my life, I always asked myself how many people could strike a paper match with one hand and then I felt a whole lot better.

"Your neighbor say anything else?"

"Just that one night Muldaur was over there and Oates walked in on them."

"Walked in on what exactly?"

"He isn't sure. But he said later that Oates told him he pulled a gun on Muldaur and ordered him out of the house."

The cigarette was helping to wake me up. So was the information.

Pam Oates had seemed so open, so forthright. You always feel betrayed on a personal level when somebody you arrogantly dismissed as a simpleton proves not to be a simpleton at all. Because that makes you the simpleton, doesn't it?

"The way I see it," Kenny Thibodeau said. He was wearing his deerstalker hat, no doubt about it. "Oates kills Muldaur over Pam and then kills Courtney when Courtney won't give him the blackmail money he was giving Muldaur."

"How did you find out about the blackmail?"

"It's all over town."

"Oh, great. Poor Dierdre."

"Huh?"

"Never mind. Thanks for the call, Kenny. This is helpful."

I got some coffee going, took a shower, and got dressed in the lightest clothes I could find. It was already in the mid-eighties.

It was Sunday morning but I went to the office anyway.

The place had a Sunday feel. Lonely, and making me feel a little like an intruder in my own place. I went through Sunday's mail. No money, nothing of interest.

I walked over to Monahan's for my second breakfast

in less than ten hours. Scrambled eggs and a piece of toast. I was having my after-meal cigarette and coffee when Kylie came in.

She had a grin that could've lit up the Holland Tunnel.

She was dressed in a pink sleeveless blouse, pink pedal pushers, white flats. Her lustrous hair and eyes were set off nicely. She ordered coffee and took out her pack of Cavaliers.

"Well, you still married?"

"Not only still married. More married than ever." She sounded like a convert to some cult religion that promised nothing less than perpetual bliss.

"I'm jealous."

"You'll find somebody, McCain."

"That's what they keep telling me."

"You could have had me if Chad hadn't really come through last night."

I'd never seen her this happy. In a strange way, she was a bit scary.

"He told me about every one of his slips."

"His slips?"

"Turns out, this girl he's seeing now, she wasn't the first one. You know, on the side."

"Ah."

"There've been at least five others."

"At least?"

"He isn't sure. He said it depends on how you count. A couple of them, he didn't go all the way, strictly speaking."

"The considerate devil."

"And I've made mistakes, too, McCain."

"Not like he has."

She thought a moment. "This is where being a Catholic would be nice."

"Huh?"

"I could just go to confession and I'd feel better."

"Maybe Jews should have confession."

"Nah, it wouldn't work."

"Why not?"

"Jews are so guilty about everything, if we had confession we'd be in there eighteen hours a day."

I laughed.

She thought some more. She let me tune in in mid-sentence. "But that's all behind him now. He said to think of him as the new Chad."

"New and improved."

"I know you're cynical about this, McCain. But don't Catholics believe in redemption? People do change, you know."

"So you really think he's changed?"

"He's going into Iowa City today—he's already left, in fact—and breaking it off with this girl. Complete break. And then we're going on a three-day trip together. Maybe get married again in some little chapel up in Door County."

"That's the prettiest part of Wisconsin." California has the most variegated and spectacular scenery but for sheer beauty, I'll still take Wisconsin.

She grabbed my hand. Squeezed.

"Thanks for getting me through this, McCain."

"My pleasure." And it was.

I had a perky erection just sitting here next to her. It's always nice when somebody who's fun, bright, and great company also stirs your groin.

"So when do you leave?"

"Tonight. Soon as he gets back from Iowa City.

He's got a bunch of work he's got to wrap up there. And I've got stuff at the paper. Say, there isn't anything new on the Muldaur thing, is there?"

"Not so's you'd notice."

"It goes without saying that I'll be the first reporter you tell, right?"

I leaned over and kissed her on the cheek. She had thrilling flesh. "You'll be the first, Toots."

SEVENTEEN

I WAS HEADING OUT to talk to Pam Oates when I saw her husband's truck parked at Clymer's Seed & Feed. Clymer's sold just about every kind of seed and feed for farm and animal life there was. The Chamber of Commerce always mentioned Clymer's because it was a good draw for small communities nearby. And when people drove their pickups and panel trucks in to buy things at Clymer's, they just naturally spent money other places in town, too.

The place was long, narrow, and sunny and contained various scents that combined to form an earthy perfume. The one thing Clymer's did that some folks objected to was open on Sundays. But the place was crowded, so not everybody took offense.

I saw Bill Oates in the back, talking to a salesman about cattle feed. Special varieties were hard to come by at the co-op, I was told. They sold only the most popular brands and types.

I didn't want him to see me. He wasn't going to like what I was about to do.

The salesman was a kid named Bobby Fowler. This would be a summer job. He'd be a freshman at the university in a few weeks. He looked like 1953: crew cut, high pants, checkered short-sleeved shirt buttoned all the way to the top. He even had a plastic pencil holder jammed into his pocket, with a variety of pens and pencils stuck in it. Still the acne problem. Still the teeth problem. Crooked and unsightly.

I'd always liked him. He used to come by the house on his ancient, clattering Schwinn with the ancient, worn saddlebags and the big light on the handlebars. He had this obvious and tormented crush on my sister, Ruthie. She was way too pretty and cool for him. Never cruel to him, the way the other kids were, but she wasn't going to sacrifice anything for him, either. The Ruthie McCains of the world just didn't go out with the Bobby Fowlers.

After talking with Kenny Thibodeau, I realized that one person who had a reason for killing both Muldaur and Courtney was indeed Bill Oates. Muldaur had been sleeping with his wife and Courtney did in fact represent an income source to him. Not inconceivable that he knew about Dierdre and Courtney. Maybe Muldaur had told Pam and Pam had told her husband.

And maybe Oates had poisoned Muldaur, taken care of Courtney, and then planted the rat poison in Sara Hall's garage.

And if he was going to buy rat poison, Clymer's would be a good place to do it.

Oates was talkative. They spoke for another five minutes. Bobby kept tapping the feed bags the way he'd seen the more experienced salesmen do, and once he even put a brown oxford on the edge of a bag and shot his trouser cuff. The way the pros did.

Oates didn't look especially impressed. He was not, apparently, hearing what he wanted to hear, because every few minutes or so he'd shake his head and look unhappy. Not angrily, just stubbornly. *You ain't im-*

pressin' me, kid, and you might as well quit tryin'.
Something like that.

Oates finally left and I walked over to Bobby.

"Gee, hi, Sam."

"Hi, Bobby. You getting ready for college?"

"Yeah." He smiled. "I guess there're a lot of chicks there." Those teeth were killers.

"There sure were when I went there."

The pain came up fast and without warning, luminous in the depths of his eyes like tumors. "So how's Ruthie?"

Fitzgerald was always doing that in his stories. Having some guy think about some girl who'd deserted or betrayed him long, long years ago. But when he thought of her the pain was still fresh as a knife slash.

"Getting along. She put the kid up for adoption."

"Yeah. She was too young for a kid, anyway."

I guess that's why I'd always liked Bobby. He had his Ruthie McCain and I had my beautiful Pamela Forrest. All The Sad Young Men, as Fitzgerald titled one of his collections.

"She seeing anybody there in Chicago?"

"I don't think so. She's getting her high-school diploma at night and working during the day."

"That's great."

"Yeah."

"Tell her I said hi."

"I sure will."

He glanced around nervously, as if he were about to share a nuclear secret with me. "She ever visits, tell her I'd like to see her."

"I'll do that."

And then he said, "I'm gettin' my teeth fixed."

And I, of course, did the social and polite and really

bullshit thing and said, "Your teeth? What's wrong with your teeth?"

"They're all kinda snaggly and stuff. Got all that green stuff stuck in the crevices and all. Anyway, my cousin Pete is gonna be a dentist in Cedar Rapids, and he says he can fix me up. Says he needs the practice and'll do it for nothin'."

"Gosh, that's great, Bobby."

"You could mention that to Ruthie, too."

"I'll be sure to." Then: "You know, Bobby, I could use a little favor."

"Sure, Sam."

And if I do it will you be sure to tell Ruthie? I was using him. I had to.

"Does the store here keep records of the poisons it sells?"

"Some of them."

"Strychnine?"

"Oh, the Muldaur guy, huh?"

"Yeah."

"I read Mickey Spillane all the time. I love murder stuff."

It was a town full of blooming private eyes.

"But didn't Cliffie arrest Sara Hall?"

"He did. But she didn't do it."

"You figure Cliffie's wrong again?"

"I figure Cliffie's always wrong."

A grin. With those teeth.

"So if she didn't do it, who did?"

"Bobby, listen, I can't really talk about it, you know?"

"Mike Hammer's like that." Bobby tapped his head. "Keeps it all right up here in his head. Won't even share it with the cops. No matter how often they beat him up." Then: "But there might be another way to check on the poison."

"How?"

"If the person who bought it has a credit account with us."

"Say, I never thought of that."

"So whose file should I look in?"

I half-whispered.

"You were just talking to him."

"Oates? Bill Oates? You think Bill Oates did it?"

A megaphone couldn't have made his voice any louder.

"Gosh, Bobby. You think Mike Hammer would bellow out somebody's name like that?"

He blushed.

"Damn, I'm sorry, Sam."

"Could you check in Oates' file?"

"Sure. But it'll take me a few minutes."

While he was gone, I walked around. I'm the same way in feed and seed stores that I am in hardware stores. They unman me. Grown-up men know how to use hammers, nails, saws, two-by-fours and lintels. And just so do grown-up men know about soil and plant life and mulch and peat moss. In fact, those are manly code words, mulch and peat moss and two-by-fours and lintels.

I'm not a grown-up man. I walk around with holes in my socks and the elastic loose on my shorts and I can't get it right with a girl yet—except maybe for Mary Travers, but I've already screwed her life up enough and don't want to do it any more damage— and I know my twenty-fifth birthday's coming early next year. But I won't be any older. Not where it counts. Not in the head. Not in the soul. You know that Fa-

mous Artists School where you can write away and
they teach you how to draw? There should be a Famous Grown-Ups School where real true adults give
you all their secrets for being an adult. The only comforting thing is, I'm not alone. You see guys with white
hair and slumped-over backs walking around who say
things just as callow and stupid as the things I say.
They need to join the Famous Grown-Ups School, too.

I tried faking it.

I walked around and tapped an important hand on a
mulch bag and said to a passing couple, "Mulch. Good
old mulch. How can you go wrong with mulch?"

I think they went and called the mental hospital
eighteen miles due west of us.

I did the same thing with peat moss. Except I sniffed
it. An elderly lady named Florence Windom was
watching me and said, "Are you smelling that, Mc-
Cain?"

"Yes'm."

"Smelling peat moss? I never heard of such a
thing."

"Most people don't know about it. That's why they
always end up buying the bad stuff."

"I'll have to tell Merle. Thanks for the tip, Mc-
Cain."

I would probably have done some more walking
around—I was trying to combine strolling and swag-
gering which, when you think about it, isn't all that
easy to do—when young Bobby came back.

"Strychnine," he said.

"Is there a date when he bought it?"

He gave me the date.

"That's two days *after* Muldaur was killed."

"Is that bad?"

"Yeah, it is, Bobby. And I'm not even sure what it means."

"You going to ask him about it?"

"I sure am, Bobby."

It was then I saw that the couple I'd made the mulch remark to had joined Florence Windom in whispering together and pointing at me. And smirking.

You try and give people a little good advice, and what do you get?

EIGHTEEN

THE BLACK CARS BEGAN appearing late that Sunday morning. The men ran to type. Trim, sunglassed, somehow foreign in style of clothing and manner. But then anybody in these parts who didn't buy their suits at Sears or J.C. Penney's looked sort of foreign. A number of them carried walkie-talkies. Secret Service.

The Vice President of the United States was about to visit our fair town.

They were scoping out the business district. An election being in progress, Nixon would certainly take the opportunity to speak to The People as well as visit his friend the Judge.

Since the scouts seemed to be concentrating on the town square area, I assumed that this was where he'd be giving his speech. Pockets of people had gathered to watch the agents at work. There'd be talk of this for a long time and by the time a year or so had passed everything would have been quadrupled. The number of agents, the number of black cars, the number of walkie-talkies. One tale-teller would throw in a few submachine guns and another tale-teller would add a sinister-looking foreign type lurking around the edges of the town square, and yet another tale-teller would invent a gun battle between a lurking foreign type and an All-American agent and there you'd go, a tale for the ages. I sometimes get the feeling that this is how most history gets written.

I stayed around twenty minutes talking with people on the street corner about the invasion Black River Falls was undergoing. Dick Nixon was a popular man out here. This was a moderate state, politically, and after the siege of the Taft and McCarthy factions at the last GOP convention—as one guy on CBS said, ''It sounded like Germany in 1931''—Nixon looked pretty moderate, hard as that was for most Democrats to recognize.

The ragtop made the drive enjoyable. I took the long way, the blacktop out along the river. There were a couple of homemade sailboats arcing against the line of horizon and they sure were pretty. A skywriting plane was again championing the virtues of Pepsi-Cola. And half a dozen teenage couples strolled hand-in-hand along the riverbank.

No sign of any trucks or cars at the Oates place.

I pulled up, killed the engine. Got out.

Even with the cows and the chickens, there was a sense of desolation to this acreage. The hill people usually gave this impression—living isolated and transient—whole groups of them had been known to pick up and move away overnight. Gypsy-like.

I knocked a few mandatory knocks and got in response the mandatory silence. The sun was helping me sweat off a few pounds. I got my handkerchief out and started mopping my brow farmer-style. Farmers know how to look natural daubing themselves with their hankies. City folk always look a little fussy.

I walked down to the garage-like shed at the bottom of the slant, scattering squawking, feather-flying chickens as I went. Turds crunched beneath my shoe leather.

In the hazy distance I could see a green John Deere in a cornfield. Nice afternoon to get a nice new paperback and a couple of Pepsis and sit out in the shade of an oak.

Sheds and garages always fascinate me. I like the ancient, musty smells of them—most of them, anyway—and the particular kind of shadows they cast and the attic-like jumble of items you find in them.

Oates had tools here, and newly sawed lumber that smelled like the old days when I was a kid and my dad built things in the garage. There were small piles of wood dust on the floor and a worktable covered with hammers, nails, screwdrivers, and four different saws.

But it was the other things that interested me.

People keep old stuff for no good reason. Maybe they think it's bad luck to give it away. Or maybe they're just sentimental about it. But how attached can you get to toasters that don't work, a wooden case of cobwebbed Coca-Cola empties, a stack of *Liberty* magazines that innumerable animal species had gone not only number one but number two on as well, car tires worn beyond repair, a rusty lawn mower, a baby carriage with most of the hood ripped away? These weren't the kinds of things you'd press into a scrapbook. But they were the kinds of things some people kept in their garages.

I heard them coming. All that rattle of truck metal was hard to miss.

I had to make a calculation. Was there time for me to make it to my car and get away?

Probably not.

Was there any good place to hide?

Not that I could get to in time.

I'd have to make do with the shed here.

My best bet looked to be a stack of slashed tires in the rear of the place.

The truck clattered to a stop.

A truck door in need of oiling resisted opening.

Pam Oates said, "Be careful. He might have a gun this time."

She was right, actually. This time, I did have a gun. And I'd come to resent Oates enough that I sure wouldn't mind using it. Not shooting him. I wasn't certain I could shoot anybody except in a moment of true self-defense. But I sure wouldn't mind pistol-whipping him for a few days.

"You don't worry about me, woman," Oates said. "You worry about him."

He canvassed the yard and the other outbuildings. He called out my name several times, as if he were summoning his dog.

You know how in books and movies and TV shows nobody ever has to go to the bathroom or shift in their hiding place because their butt goes to sleep. Or has to sneeze. Or fart. But in fact, it's stuff like that that gives you away. I was packed in so tight that if I moved, the stacked tires just might come tumbling down.

I mention this because of the bee.

Okay, it wasn't exactly a bee, it was a small-to-middling yellow jacket. It didn't even look especially fierce. I mean, you can run into some yellow jackets that are so big and bold they give you the finger and moon you before they sting you.

This one seemed to be just sort of flying around, taking in the scenery. Maybe it was on yellow jacket vacation.

It landed on a tire above my head, it dropped onto

the rotting wooden wall behind me, and then hovered above my nose.

Yes, my nose. It's a little Irish nose and while I don't especially like it, it's all I've got.

So there were a couple things annoying about the yellow jacket hovering there.

One, with such a clear field, its sting was going to hurt like hell and probably cause me to carom off the wall and knock the tires over.

And two, the sting could really be ugly on my face. You're surprised I'm vain? I have to admit that Robert Ryan probably wasn't—or Roy Rogers or Gene Autry if you want to go back to my boyhood—but I was. I didn't want a string swelling up on my little Mick schnoz. And what if it were to get infected? Then I'd have this huge disfigurement in the center of my face.

So, please don't sit on my nose, Mr. Yellow Jacket. Please don't sit on my nose.

It didn't give me the finger. And it didn't moon me. But it most definitely sat on my nose.

And when it did, I did just what I'd been afraid I'd do.

I lurched forward, hoping the movement would shoo the insect away before it had time to insert its stinger.

Well, I avoided getting strung, all right. But in the process, I knocked over the highest half of the tires. They didn't crash, they kinda *whumpfed* to the dirt floor, but the *whumpfing* was sufficient to bring Bill Oates on the run.

I ran to the front of the garage, pressed myself flat against the small wall inside.

In the quiet, I heard his feet slapping against the summer-burnt grass, coming faster and faster, closer and closer. And I heard the rattlesnakes.

I wasn't sure where they were. Somewhere not too far away. Hissing and rattling. I could easily, too easily, picture them in their cage. The *whumpfing* (yes, it is fun to say that word, isn't it?) must have stirred them.

When Bill Oates came racing into the garage, all I had to do was suddenly inject my leg into his forward-motion path. He hit the floor, making much the same sound the tires had. The shotgun he was toting didn't misfire.

His hand flicked out quickly to grab the weapon but I stopped it with the heel of my shoe. I put the full weight of my body on his knuckles. One of them made a cracking sound. It was most pleasurable to hear. He made a pitiful noise in his throat.

"Where're the snakes?"

"What?"

"The rattlers. Where are they?"

"Out back-a the garage, why?"

"We're going to pay them a visit."

"What you're up to, McCain?"

His voice now had real pain in it. I decided I hadn't broken anything, after all. Just moved things around a little. I stepped down even harder.

"You're going to tell me that you bought strychnine at Clymer's two days after Muldaur was murdered and then planted it in Sara Hall's garage."

"I'm not gonna tell you anything."

"Which leads me to believe that you didn't kill Muldaur or Courtney. But somebody you care about did. And now you're protecting her."

I took my foot off his hand.

"Get up."

He didn't, of course. He just kind of lay there wriggling his hurting hand around, working it like a piece of equipment that was on the fritz.

Then I went and stepped on it again.

He clearly wanted to deny me the satisfaction of giving me the big dramatic scream. But he did make one of those real strange throat noises.

"Get up."

This time he did, using his good hand to swat away some of the floor dirt he'd gotten on his Osh Kosh overalls.

We'd just left the shadows of the garage when Pam Oates opened the screen door at the back of the house and said, "You all right, Bill?"

"You just go on inside, woman," he snapped.

"You ever think I worry about you, Bill?"

"Were you worried about me those times you were with Muldaur?"

This was a long way from the home life depicted on "Father Knows Best" every week. Oates hated her and loved her. He needed to forgive her and it was obvious he couldn't. Not yet. Maybe someday. Sometimes, something happens that you can't forgive. And it kills you because you can't forgive. You drag it along with you your whole life and remember it at odd moments and no matter how old you get, that one thing still retains its fresh and vital pain. And a part of you knows that the other person has gone on and probably never thinks about it at all.

She closed the screen door quietly and disappeared behind it.

"She killed him," I said, "because she wanted to end it and he didn't. And then she tried to blackmail Courtney—give you two enough money to go on the run—but he said no and she got mad and stabbed him.''

''You should write books, McCain.''

Moving, all the time moving. Along the side of the garage in the blistering, bleaching sun.

The rattlers were getting loud now. My mental picture of them was getting clearer and clearer.

We reached the back edge of the garage and there they were. Same cage. Same number of rattlers. Out there in the scathing sun. As much as I could, I felt sorry for the damned things.

I prodded Oates forward with the barrel of my .45.

''Now we're going to find out how holy you are, Mr. Oates.''

''What're you talking about, McCain?''

''I noticed that you never handle the snakes yourself. Not the night Muldaur died, not the time you tried to force me to shove my hand into the cage. Now it's your turn.''

''Oh, no. I ain't stickin' my hand in there.''

''Sure you are, Oates. Or I'm going to shoot you in the arm. And if you still won't do it, I'm going to shoot you in the leg. And I'm gonna tell Cliffie I did it in self-defense. He hates you people even more than he hates me. So he'll go along.''

''No,'' he said. ''No. You can't do this.''

All his mountain swagger was gone.

He glanced over his shoulder at me.

''I have nightmares about those snakes, McCain. I really do.''

''I thought you were so holy.''

''Nobody's holy, McCain.''

''Then how do some people handle these snakes?''

"They're just lucky, I guess. Please don't make me handle them, all right?"

"Then tell me the truth about the strychnine."

"I can't do that, McCain. No matter what. Just please don't—"

This could've been a briar-patch routine. Please don't throw me in that briar patch, oh, my, don't. But I doubted it. His eyes were starting to look frantic, the stigma of real bowel-wrenching fear.

Looked like he was going to tell me all the things I wanted to hear.

We reached the cage.

The rattlers didn't look any prettier or any friendlier.

"Reach down and open the lid."

"I—can't do it, McCain."

"Well, you'll have to do one or the other."

He just shook his head.

I surprised both of us by firing a shot that missed his head by about three inches.

He jerked, sobbed. He was too fierce for jerking and sobbing. Or so I'd thought. You want bad guys to be bad in every way and that included not responding to stress the way we common folk do.

This wasn't any briar patch.

Between my bullet and the snakes and the burden of holding his secrets, he was in a bad, bad way.

I clubbed him on the side of the head with my .45. Got him hard on the ear. And then I changed gun hands and planted a fist into his stomach. What he did was puke. Not a lot. But his whole stomach, not so much from my punch but from all the tension he was feeling, backed up on him.

This time when I hit him on the side of the head,

he dropped to his knees right next to the snake cage, which is where I'd wanted him in the first place.

"Open it," I said.

The snakes were as crazy at this moment as he was, and he knew it.

"No."

I kicked him in the hip.

"Cast your burden on the Lord, and He will sustain you." He was starting in with the Bible again. He was begging the Lord to get him out of here and I couldn't really blame him.

"Open it up, Oates."

"For thou hast been to me a fortress and a refuge in my day of distress."

"Open it up, Oates."

Either he'd run out of Bible quotes or he'd finally realized that he didn't have much choice here. He put his long, shaking hand to the lid of the cage.

And that was when somebody shoved a metal rod into the base of my back.

"I want you off our land, Mr. McCain. You don't have no call to treat a man like you're treating him."

"You should've seen the way he treated me, Mrs. Oates."

Oh, yeah, well he punched me first, Sister Mary Francis. I'd used that line all the way through grade school and it was nice to know that a variation of it still applied.

"I just want you to go. I just want all this over with."

"Somebody killed two men, Mrs. Oates. I'm wondering if it was you."

"Don't say nothin' to him," Oates said.

"Maybe Courtney was killed because he'd run out

of money to pay the blackmailer," I said, "and the blackmailer was afraid Courtney might go to see Cliffie."

"You heard what I said," Oates snapped. "Don't say nothin' to him."

So he was inclined to see things the way I did. He thought his wife killed the men and he had planted the strychnine to make it appear that Sara Hall was the guilty one.

"You need to leave now, Mr. McCain," she said.

I didn't have much choice.

He took the rifle from her and sent her to the house and then, after dropping my gun in the pocket of his overalls, he walked me back to the car.

"She let the Devil take her a few times," he said, as if I'd just accused the missus of something. "But she has cleansed herself since. She ain't even afraid of the snakes, which shames me. The man of the house shouldn't show fear. But I just can't stand those things."

"She killed those men, Oates."

"You don't know that for a fact."

"Maybe not. Though I think you do."

The sun was so hot not even the dust wanted to rise when an old truck passed by in front of the yard. I was betting the chickens wished they had electric fans.

"You don't trouble us no more," he said when he reached the ragtop.

"You really think things're this easy, Oates?"

"You don't dwell on things, sometimes the good Lord just takes them away."

"The good Lord may but then Cliffie brings them right back."

"You can't prove anything. And anyway, you know

how them Sykeses don't like to be showed up. You tell him about that strychnine and he'll say 'so what?' Strychnine is sold all the time. He's got Sara Hall all zeroed in on and nothin's gonna change his mind.''

Oates was probably right. I didn't know for a fact that Pam had killed anybody. I just had a suspicion that he had a suspicion that his wife had killed the two men. But that was surmise, not fact.

I got in the Ford and did a little backside-dancing. The seats, back and bottom, were blast-furnace hot. The steering wheel was probably going to brand my palms for life.

"You get away from here now," he said. "And you don't come back."

The seats were still scorching when I got back to town.

NINETEEN

THE DRIVE-IN WAS showing a Vincent Price "Triple Terror" feature that night. His lisp didn't do much for me but he was effective in a hammy sort of way. They advertised this in "spooky" lettering on their big sign out front. That sounded good. Lots of buttery popcorn from the concession stand, a nice breeze off the surrounding cornfields, and my arm around any girl I could find who'd go out with me. A bachelor my age in a small Iowa town has slim pickings. Girls are either married off or knocked up by the time they reach twenty; by twenty-five they're having baby number three or four. I would have daydreamed about taking the beautiful Pamela Forrest tonight but she'd never have gone to the drive-in. She would have called it "uncouth," a word she picked up from an old Bette Davis movie we saw together on TV one night.

I didn't recognize the car in my drive.

The garage door was open, Mrs. Goldman's car was gone. Meaning this gink didn't have sense or courtesy enough not to block her when she came back home.

The car was a forest-green MG. It looked dashing in the way of many things British. That's one thing the Brits have got all over us, the dashing stuff. We have better cooking, prettier girls, and a higher class of rock stars. But they've got a corner on the dashing stuff.

I parked at the curb and walked around back. He was sitting on my steps, smoking a cigarette with one hand, patting his hair with another. Maybe there was an invisible photographer somewhere about to take his picture. America's favorite unknown literary genius. Just ask him.

When he looked at me, he frowned. "This wasn't easy for me to come here. I want you to know that."

He sounded as if he wanted me to pin a medal for valor on him.

"You could always leave," I said. "Like right now, for instance."

"Let's get one thing straight. I think you're a two-bit hayseed lawyer who works for a fascist judge in an intolerable little burg."

"OK, now I'll tell *you* what I think of *you*."

"You didn't let me finish. You see me as an untalented, spoiled, rich boy who is cheating on a very sweet young woman who was stupid to fall in love with me in the first place and is even dumber to stay with me now that she knows the truth. At least part of the truth."

"Part of the truth?"

He looked suitably miserable for what he was about to say, a stage figure in his inevitable white button-down shirt and chinos.

"The truth is I've never been faithful. The day after our wedding night—in Paris, thanks to the largesse of my parents—I screwed the maid."

"The maid?"

"She was eighteen. You wouldn't have believed her tits."

"And Kylie was—"

"—out shopping."

"The old screw-the-maid-with-the-big-tits-while-the-little-woman-is-out-shopping routine. And you are ashamed of yourself, of course."

"Of course. You think I'm proud of it?"

"Yeah, I do. Because there was a little smirk in your voice when you told me about it. You like being the conqueror, and you know what? The big lug just can't help himself. He's just a charming rogue, isn't he? There's just enough of me like you to recognize it, Chad. But where I'm not like you is that I'd never do it while I was married. I'd at least get a divorce before I went back to chasing."

He was wringing his hands now. He didn't know how to wring his hands worth a damn. His hand-wringing made him look prissy.

"That's why I'm here."

"I'm not following."

"I'm here to ask you a favor."

You know how things come clear all of a sudden and you just know, almost word for word, what you're about to hear, but you reject it because you don't think that anybody would have the arrogance to ask?

"Don't ask me," I said.

I dug out a Lucky and got it going.

"You don't even know what I'm going to say."

"Sure, I do."

"All right, what is it?"

"You're going to ask me to go find Kylie and tell her that you've decided you're in love with your little undergrad after all and that it's time—painful as it is, and you're sorry as all hell—to get a divorce."

I had to give him his courage.

Without hesitation, he said, "That's not an easy thing to ask a guy."

He wanted another medal.

"You didn't ask a guy, dip-shit. *I* asked a guy."

"Well, I guess that's sort of right. But I would've asked if you hadn't asked yourself first."

"You are a living, crawling, slimy piece of shit."

"You think I don't know it? I know I'm a bastard. And I don't even know why. I just keep falling in love. It's not just getting pussy, McCain. It really isn't. I really, truly fall in love. But it never lasts very long."

"You fell in love with the maid?"

"You're not gonna believe this—I damned near asked her to marry me."

And I felt sorry for him. I wasn't even sure why. But every once in a while you see somebody the way they really are—it only takes a second of seeing them that way—and then you can't hate them quite as much as you did. It's a curse.

Then he did me a favor and went back to his whining. "I'm jeopardizing my inheritance here, you know."

I was running out of medals to pin on this guy.

"It's funny," he said. He took out his pack of Viceroys. "My parents were against me marrying her because she was Jewish. They're not anti-Semitic or anything—Kylie's folks weren't all that hot about me marrying her, either—just that they're pretty strict Catholics and everything—but now—I mean, I've kept them up on developments and everything—now they're taking *her* part in this. They've really gotten to love her."

"That isn't hard to do."

Sudden anger. "You bastard. You did screw her that night she was here, didn't you?"

I could have told him the truth. But why? His ego

needed some grief. In my best mature voice, I said, "That's for me to know and you to find out."

"God," he said, miserably. "You can't trust anybody these days." And then—to give him at least a smidge of credit here—he said, "I guess that's pretty ironic coming from me, huh? About not being able to trust anybody, I mean."

"I won't tell her for you, Chad."

He started talking to himself. Angled his head away. Took a deep drag on his smoke and began to ramble. "You know what I'm really scared of? Looking into her eyes when I tell her. You ever see her eyes when you hurt her feelings? She looks like this devastated little girl."

He was right.

"And I don't want to put that hurt in her eyes anymore. I've been doing it night after night for a month now. I haven't just walked away, McCain. You have to give me that, anyway. I know I've gone back and forth between the two of them but it's only because I don't want to hurt Kylie. Hell, I've known for a long time that we had a shit marriage. We never should've been married in the first place. We're just too combustible."

He was starting to persuade me and he knew it.

"She'll still want to see you," I said.

He looked at me, done with his reverie.

"Oh, I know. But she'll know the situation. I won't explain that to her because you'll already have covered it." Then: "I won't even care if you sleep with her."

"You pimping for her now? I hate to tell you this, Chad, but you don't have the right to hand her out like candy."

"You jerk. You know what I mean."

"No, I don't know what you mean. Now get off my steps."

"So you'll do it?"

"You slimy, crawling, stinking piece of shit."

"So you'll do it, McCain? Will ya, please? Will ya?"

"You vain, pompous, arrogant—"

"So you'll do it?"

"Yeah," I said, "you rotten bastard, I'll do it."

SHE WASN'T HOME and she wasn't home and she wasn't home. I kept trying her every ten minutes. I wanted to get it over with. I dragged the phone with its long extension cord over to the couch so that I could lie down and watch "Science Fiction Theater." It had been on back when I was still a teenager. It was funny how I was already nostalgic for a pastime. How can you be nostalgic when you're only twenty-four? But it was the old shows and the old songs and the old sights—the way the shadows of the trees played on the river; the deserted baseball park where you could see advertisements on the fence for business that didn't exist anymore; the Catholic school where I'd pined so arduously for the beautiful Pamela far across town at public school—much as I liked Kerouac and art films and *Evergreen Review* and Lenny Bruce—I already missed the simpler times behind me. And "Science Fiction Theater" with the ultimate father figure, Truman Bradley, was part of those simpler times.

She called.

"He isn't here."

"I know. You need to come over here."

"What?"

"Please. Just get in your car and come over."

"Oh, God, this is going to be bad, isn't it, Mc-Cain?"

"Please, Kylie. Just come over."

"He couldn't even face me himself, could he?"

"Right away," I said. "Please." And hung up.

She was at my door in under ten minutes. Her knock was exceptionally loud. I learned this was because she knocked on the door with a full fifth of Jack Daniels. In her other hand she carried a suitcase. A big one.

No sign she'd been crying. No sign of trembling. No sign of anger. This was scary.

I took her suitcase.

"You want a drink?" I said.

"Please. You mind if we put on some music?"

"Anything in particular?"

"You pick."

"Been listening to this blues guy. Oscar Brown, Jr."

"Fine," she said.

She got her drink and she got Oscar Brown, Jr.

She sat at one end of the couch with her lovely legs stretched out across my lap. She wore blue walking shorts and a white T-shirt.

"He tell you he was leaving me?"

"Uh-huh."

"He say he was in love with her?"

"Uh-huh."

"He say he couldn't face me because he 'didn't want to put any more hurt' in my eyes?"

"Yeah. Some kinda bullshit like that. He probably thinks it's a good line."

"He does. He thinks all his lines are good lines."

"And by the way, thanks for telling me what I was supposed to tell you. I was sorta nervous about how I'd say it."

"I almost told him I was pregnant."

"You're pregnant?"

"No. But it would've made him suffer. This way he just gets to walk away."

She finished her drink in three gulps. Then swung her legs off me and stood up.

"You ready for another one?"

"Not yet," I said.

"I'm going to make a stiff one."

"The night's young."

She actually smiled. "Yes, McCain, and so are we."

She poured about half a glass full of sour mash, ran a silver slip of tap water into it, added a couple ice cubes from the fridge, and then came back, bringing those wonderful long legs with her.

When they were once again inhabiting my lap, she said, "Tonight's the night we sleep together, Mc-Cain."

"Probably not."

"C'mon, McCain, I've got to sleep with you tonight."

"Because he's sleeping with *her* tonight."

"No, because I want to sleep with *you*."

"You like me. I like you. We're friends. That part's true. But the reason you want to sleep with me is because of her."

"Well, maybe part of the reason."

"Most of the reason."

"Maybe fifty percent of the reason," she said.

"Maybe eighty percent of the reason."

"Maybe fifty-five percent of the reason."

We listened to Oscar Brown, Jr.

"Boy, this drink's really getting to me," she said.

"That's probably more booze than you've had in

your entire life—right there in that one drink. Nobody says you've got to drink it.''

She set it down on the coffee table.

''Wow. I'm woozy.''

She laid her head back against the arm of the couch. Closed her eyes.

''Would you dance with me?'' she said.

''I thought you were woozy.''

''I'm all right now.''

''You're a dancer, huh?''

''Not really. I mean, I used to dance with my sister sometimes when we watched 'American Bandstand.' And I danced in high school the few times the boys would ask me. They wanted to slow-dance with girls with big breasts so that let me out.'' Pause. ''I want you to hold me, McCain, I really *need* you to hold me, and dancing's a good way to do that.''

''How about some Nat King Cole?''

''Perfect. I need to go to the bathroom first, though.''

I had an album of ballads by Cole. It was Mathis or Cole or Darin when I wanted ballads. Hearing Bobby Rydell ruin a Jerome Kern song wasn't something I dealt with very well.

I heard the glass smashing in the bathroom and a terrible thought filled my mind. The jagged glass from the Skippy peanut-butter jar I kept my toothbrush in—ripping across her wrists.

I lunged for the door.

She'd been emotional, after all—suicidally so.

The door swung open and there she was.

''Dammit, I broke your glass, McCain. You had it sitting right on the edge of the sink and I thought it wouldn't fall off. But you had some kind of greasy stuff all over it.''

''Hair oil. I probably picked the glass up after I put the hair oil on. Greasy kid stuff, as they say in the ads.''

''Hair oil, then. Anyway, when I picked it up, it slid right through my fingers. Get me a dustpan and a broom and I'll clean it up.'' She fixed me with a sharp eye. ''And it wasn't because I was drinking, either.''

''I didn't say anything.''

''Yeah, but it's what you were thinking.''

''Guilty as charged, I guess.''

She looked so bedraggled and exasperated just then, her hair sort of mussed and her face damp from the heat and her clothes a little mussed, she just looked so damned sweet and lost and sad and nice and girly and true and just plain wonderful that I leaned forward and touched my lips to hers.

I forced my eager arms to stay put.

I said, ''I'll get the broom and the dustpan.''

A few minutes later, we were dancing.

''This is nice,'' she said.

''It sure is.''

We were listening to ''Lost April'' and it was great, dancing there in the living-room of my apartment. I turned the light off. A quarter moon hung in a pane of glass and a coyote cried in growing flower-scented darkness. This was kind of a medical procedure for both of us. A healing, if you will. It had been way too long since I'd held a woman and way too long since this particular woman had been held by a man she trusted. It wouldn't last long—dawn would turn us back into our real selves—but for now we were sha-dowshapes and nothing more.

"Is it all right if I kiss your neck, McCain? Because if I don't I'll start crying about you-know-who."

"Well, in that case, because it involves you-know-who, I guess I don't have much choice do I?"

One tiny little peck on my neck and I set a land speed record for getting an erection.

We got tighter.

I thought of Groucho's old gag line, "If I held you any tighter, I'd be behind you."

And then we were kissing. And I do mean kissing. And thrusting. And rubbing. And stroking. And kissing and thrusting even harder. And then rubbing and stroking even harder.

"I want to if you want to," I said.

"Well, I want to if *you* want to," she said.

All this said in great swooping gasps on both our parts.

And then we started dancing at a slight eastward angle, toward the bed.

I could see over her shoulders into the bedroom.

Tasha, Crystal, and Tess seemed to sense what was about to happen.

They jumped off the bed as if it were a sinking ocean liner.

And then we reached the bed and then—

"THANKS," SHE SAID when we were all finished.

"Are you crazy. Thank *you!*"

"I'm not that great a lover, McCain."

"Well, neither am I."

"You were pretty good."

"Well, look who's talking. You were pretty good yourself."

"At least we're being honest."

SAVE THE LAST DANCE FOR ME

"Honesty is always the best policy." I guess that's the myth of Stranger Sex. The fury of it is great but sex is actually better—at least for me—after you've been together a few times. Get to know what to do, what not to do, when to do it, when not to…need I go on?

But I was already wondering if we hadn't been a mite hasty about being perfectly honest about our first experience. We'd been expecting a Technicolor and Cinemascope musical. What we'd gotten was a nice, lusty B second feature in black-and-white on a regular-size screen.

And no reassurance.

And I think we both needed reassurance.

"You're not telling me I am a great lover and I'm not telling you you are a great lover."

"Yeah, but you did say I was pretty good, Kylie."

"Oh, you were pretty good, all right. In fact, you were very good."

"Well, that's what I meant to say to you, too. Not that you were merely pretty good. But that you were very good."

"And so were you, McCain. Not just very good. Very, very good."

Now, that was more like it. Two verys.

"You got a smoke?" she asked.

"I thought you only smoked filters."

"I'm being European tonight, McCain. Like Simone Signor. or somebody like that. European movie stars never smoke filters."

"There's nothing more alluring than lung cancer."

I got us cigarettes and got them going and gave her hers.

"God, that breeze feels good," she said, inhaling with epic depth.

We lay inches apart on the bed. Letting the breeze balm us.

"I ever tell you what he did to me the first time I ever met him at a dance?"

"I guess not."

"Could you stand to hear about it?"

"Sure."

She rolled over and kissed me on the cheek. Her breast felt swell against my arm. "Thanks for putting up with me."

"So tell me."

"Well, we met at this dance in Manhattan, see. And we danced like every other dance together. Fast and slow. And it was obvious there was something going on. You know? So I said, 'Be sure and save the last dance for me.' And he kissed me. Right there in the middle of the floor. This big dramatic kiss. An MGM kiss. And then you know what the asshole did? He started dancing with this blonde who came in. Very Vassar, if you now what I mean. Vassar or Smith. One of those real bitch schools. And then all of a sudden he forgot me entirely. He not only danced the last dance with her, he took her home."

"So how'd you meet him again?"

"Luckily—or unluckily, as things turned out—we'd already exchanged phone numbers by that point. I called him the next day."

"What he'd say about the Vassar chick?"

"Said she was an old girlfriend and he was taking pity on her."

"That Chad, always thinking of other people."

We then proceeded to nuzzle, snuggle, cuddle,

grope, bite, nibble, lick, groan, gasp, and giggle. I was almost ready but first I said, "Need to go to the can."

"Don't be long."

"Thought I'd take a paperback in there with me."

"Har-har."

I got up and walked to the john and—since I have to reconstruct the thought process here—I guess the next few seconds went this way.

I walked into the john.

And stepped on a piece of glass we hadn't swept up. Just a sliver. But it cut me enough to remind me of the glass I kept my toothbrush in.

And when I thought of the glass, I thought of it slipping out of Kylie's hand.

And then I knew who had killed Muldaur and Courtney. Things work out that way sometimes.

She watched me as I yanked my clothes on.

"But where're you going?"

"I'll be back in less than an hour."

"You're forgetting something, McCain."

"What?"

She was already throwing herself off the bed.

"I'm a reporter, McCain. And I'm going with you."

"You don't even know where we're going."

She grinned. "Doesn't matter."

TWENTY

ON THE WAY OUT there, we stopped at the Nite Owl grocery store and bought a can of lighter fluid. Then we were back on the road and I was explaining everything to her.

Fifteen minutes later I pulled off the gravel road.

"This is the part you won't like."

"What part is that, McCain?"

"I'm going in there alone."

"That isn't fair."

"I'm acting as the investigator for Judge Whitney. You're a reporter. If Cliffie wanted to make a stink about me taking you along, he could."

"So I wait till you wave a white flag?"

"Something like that."

She leaned over and kissed me.

"I guess that makes sense."

Which made me suspicious. She took her reporter's job very seriously.

I got out of the ragtop. The moon was riding high. The prairie gleamed with moonlight. A John Deere tractor with lights in a distant field looked like a giant alien insect, like the mutated kind you always see on drive-in movie screens.

The garage resembled a jungle ruin in the shadowy light. A lost race of auto mechanics had once thrived here, sacrificing virgin Fords to the motor gods until the very degeneracy of their actions caused them to vanish utterly from the earth. There was a good chance they'd gone to Atlantis.

There was light and mountain music coming from the nearby trailer.

First, to do my good deed for the day. The Boy Scout ethic was not lost on me, even though I'd been tossed out for smoking a cigar in the back of a troop meeting. Somebody had dared me to do it and in those days a good dare was a bracing and irresistible spur.

The snakes were inside the church now. I could hear them hissing from the makeshift altar. And, as my eyes became accustomed to the gloom, see the outline of their cage.

But the snakes didn't interest me—or even especially frighten me—now.

What I wanted was the corner where all those flyers were stacked. You know, JOHN KENNEDY, SECRET RABBI.

The stack sat right next to a window. I was hoping the folks in the trailer would see the fire and come running. And there I'd be with my .45 and my accusations.

I took my can of Ronson lighter fluid and went to work. I did those babies up proud. By the time I was done, the entire four-foot stack of flyers glistened. And I was out of the giant-size can of fluid.

I struck a match and very casually tossed it on to the fliers.

Whoosh! and *Whoom!* The words you frequently see in comic book panels applied here. The things *whooshed* and *whoomed* for several full seconds, like a singer sustaining a high note.

The flames leapt in every direction, burning blue-yellow. They filled the window, too, which faced the trailer. Any eye looking causally from the trailer was bound to see—

The flames lent an ugly light to the church, a light that did not soften and flatter but revealed and scorned. All the oil marks on the walls; all the cracks and fungi on the floor; all the cobwebs collected in the high rotting corners.

But the massive painting of the angry Christ was the most startling. He was beyond anger, into hard-core psychosis. He was not my Christ—you could believe in his divinity or not, it didn't matter—a Christ of sympathy, tolerance, understanding, forgiveness. He was the dark Christ embraced by dictators of all kinds, especially the darkest dictators of all, the ministers and priests who teach their followers to hate anyone different from themselves. Anyone who doesn't believe, think, dress or behave the way they do. Any mercy or compassion this Christ had ever felt was gone now, gone utterly, as he glared down at me from the wall behind the altar.

The fire burned itself out in just a couple of minutes. Ash was all that was left.

A voice said, "I could kill you right now for trespassing, Mr. McCain."

I'd been fixated on the painting of Christ and hadn't heard them come in.

Mother and daughter. The Muldaurs.

Mom, as most Midwestern moms were wont to, carried a sawed-off shotgun.

"That's our personal property, what you just burned."

"I'll be happy to pay you for it. I just don't want it dirtying up our little town."

"What you don't want is for people to know the truth, Mr. McCain. About the Jews and the Catholics. And the niggers."

Ella just stood there in her worn gingham dress, the blue eyes of that sad pretty face not quite here with us but somewhere else. But she wasn't the soft-spoken, shy Ella she pretended to be for the people who didn't know her well. There was a hardness and a harshness in the face now; and a genuine lunacy in the eyes...

She said, "My mom's right, Mr. McCain. The Jews killed Our Lord and they won't rest until they take over the world. You probably don't even realize that several of the popes were Jews."

And what should have been funny—Jewish popes, Jewish guns in the basements of Catholic churches— wasn't funny at all. It was sorrowful. Because not long ago she'd been an innocent little girl who should have been given the chance for a full, free life. But Mama and Papa had recruited her as a soldier in their dark army. The Koreans and Chinese had nothing on these folks when it came to brainwashing. The Muldaurs had turned their daughter into a vessel of pure rage and hatred. She was beyond reasoning with. She believed all their conspiracy theories, no matter how ludicrous; even did their bidding.

"You couldn't do it yourself, so you had your daughter do it," I said.

"I *wanted* to do it, Mr. McCain. It's the sort of thing God rewards you for."

"For killing your father?"

"He'd defiled the Lord, Mr. McCain," she said.

"And so did Reverend Courtney. He had defiled the Lord just the way my pa had—with sins of the flesh."

"How'd you know it was Ella?" her mother said. She didn't sound angry or frightened. More curious than anything.

"They found some kind of ointment all over the neck of the bottle your husband drank from. I didn't make the connection till tonight—to Ella's poison ivy salve."

"You're a good detective."

"Look at her, Mrs. Muldaur. Look at her face. She shouldn't look like that. She should be a nice, ordinary teenage girl."

"Wearing tight sweaters and going all the way, I suppose, like other girls in this town, Mr. McCain?"

"That's a lot better than this, Mrs. Muldaur. I said to look at her and you didn't. Because you see it too, don't you? She's insane. That's why she doesn't feel any remorse for what she did. She killed devils, not human beings. And you and your husband were the ones who taught her to think like that."

"You kill him, Mama," the girl said. "Or I will."

For the first time, Mrs. Muldaur looked nervous, uncertain. She wasn't a killer. Her daughter was.

"We could just let him leave," Mrs. Muldaur said. "Nobody'd believe what he said."

"You know better than that, Mama. Now, either you kill him or I will."

Mrs. Muldaur hesitated. And in that moment, Ella snatched the sawed-off shotgun from her.

"You go wait outside, Mama."

"I'm not sure we should do this, honey."

"You heard what I said, Mama. Wait outside."

Her mother knew there was no sense arguing. "Honey, I just wish—"

"Go wait outside," Ella said.

Mrs. Muldaur looked down at the pocket of her dress. She slid out what appeared to be an old .38. Gripped it.

I was sure for a moment she was going to tell Ella to hand back the shotgun. But she didn't. She just looked at the handgun, turned, and quietly left the church.

"You need help," I said. "There's no point in killing me, too."

"You sound like some TV show."

"You really do need help. And there are people who can help you."

She smirked. "Jews? Catholics?" She shook her head and raised the weapon. "Those're your people, not mine."

I thought of begging but what was the point? I thought of lunging at her but what was the point of that, either? I'd just be giving her a better shot at me.

"You get up on the altar, McCain." She sort of waggled the shotgun at me. "We're going to see how holy you are."

Snakes. Somehow, it always came back to snakes with these people, that litmus test of spirituality that not even the Aztecs had been nutty enough to use.

"I'm not going to handle any snakes," I said.

"Sure you are. You just don't know it yet. Leastways, you got a chance with the snakes. Otherwise, I'll kill you right here."

She really looked like she knew what she was doing with the gun. She sighted down the barrel and said, "This ain't nothin' personal."

"God," I said, "I'm glad you said that. That makes me feel a whole lot better."

"Sarcasm is the Devil's tongue. Says so right in the Bible."

"I think there's something about not killing people in there, too, Ella."

"Depends on how you read it. Way I read it, God *wants* us to smite the sinners who won't see the one true way."

She was ready. It wasn't anything she said, anything she did. But some judgment had been reached.

It was right and just and proper to kill me. Any lingering doubts banished.

I was trying to say a prayer for myself but I was too scared to form the words.

Then I said it, the words John Wayne would never say: "I really don't want to die, Ella. It isn't your fault you turned out this way. You need to talk to somebody who can help you like I said." And then: "I'm kinda afraid to die, Ella." You'll notice how I sort of slid that "kinda" in there, taking the sting off what a teeth-rattling, knee-collapsing, sphincter-cringing coward I was.

All for naught.

"You get up on that altar or I'll kill you right here and right now."

And I knew she would.

She hitched the gun up, sighted even tighter down the barrel. Her elbow kicked slightly as she got ready to fire—

And I turned and walked up to the altar.

"Sit in the chair."

I sat in the chair.

"Mama! Mama! I need you in here!"

About now, I was wondering where Kylie was. Had Mama found her? Roughed her up?

Mama came through the door. She still had the handgun clutched tight in her fingers.

"You get up here, Mama. I need you to tie him up."

They'd reversed personalities. Daughter was now mom, and definitely in charge. And mom, a big woman rendered mousy all of a sudden, was daughter.

Mama came up to the floor in front of the altar. Ella stood next to the snake cage.

"I need you to tie him up, Mama."

"I sure wish you wouldn't do this, honey. We're in trouble enough."

Ella's voice crackled. "Not with the Lord, we're not in no trouble, Mama. Where's your faith?"

Mama muttered to herself then began walking up on to the platform. I glanced over my shoulder. A coil of rough rope lay on the rear corner of the platform. Mama, all sweat now, all great sigh, all great dead eyes, dead as the eyes of the rattlers, brought the rope over.

"Tie him up," Ella said. "Good and tight."

"You've done a great job with her, Mrs. Muldaur," I said.

Mama spat in my face. Hot, dirty spittle on my cheek.

She did me good and tight. The circulation left my upper arms and my lower legs. The only thing that could cut me loose would be a scimitar and you just couldn't hardly find any of those in a small Iowa town like this.

"There you go, hon," Mama said. No more doubts. No more regrets. She wanted to see me killed. I'd insulted her one time too many.

"Now, you go stand in the back, Mama. I know how you don't like these snakes."

"I wish I had better faith, hon," Mama said, sounding genuinely ashamed of herself. "I can't help it them things scare me."

She turned—all too gladly, it seemed—and walked back to the door in the rear of the place.

Ella set her shotgun down on the floor with great care. No need to worry about me now. I was all tied up.

The snakes had gotten the message. They were having a snake revival meeting inside the cage. While they weren't ordinarily much interested in human beings— they only struck out at us because they were as afraid of us as we were of them—they were getting ready to take all their caged frustrations out on me.

Ella went over to the cage, leaned down and did a little work on the latch holding the lid in place. She couldn't seem to get it open.

Could I be that lucky? Of course not. A couple of seconds later she flipped the latch and then opened the lid a few inches.

You could feel the energy of the rattlers. The thrust and thrum and mean intent of them. Back when our species had been only twenty inches high, we'd learned to dread and fear these creatures. And that dread stayed with us. It was with me right now.

And then she did it. The unthinkable. Just plunged her hand down inside the cage—pretty casually, really—and up came a timber rattler.

I almost felt sorry for it. The thing was in pure frenzy. Ella had obviously mastered the trick of holding it in such a way that it couldn't angle its head around to strike at her.

"Are you pure of soul, Mr. McCain?" she said. "Somehow, I doubt that you are."

She carried the snake over to me. Wriggling, wrenching, wrestling its body around in mid-air—and furious—she slapped the lower third of the rattler against my face. I made some kind of undignified sound of terror. I jerked up in my seat, bringing the chair with me.

"You're sure a 'fraidy cat, Mr. McCain." She said this clinically, as if surprised that anybody my age could possibly fear rattlesnakes this much.

Then she got serious.

Gripping the snake tighter than ever, she brought it even closer, touching the lower part of it to my neck.

"I never was able to get one of these things around anybody's neck," she said, again with great cold loony dispassion. "Maybe I'll have better luck with you."

This time I didn't try to come up out of my chair. I knew better. I had to be as still as I could be.

The rattle. The insane hissing.

Ella taking the snake and starting to wind it around my neck.

And then her mama fell face forward.

I'd been concentrating on Ella's large body but she moved out of the way—trying to get the snake to coil better around my neck—and it was just then that Mama hit the floor. Heart attack? I couldn't think of anything that could fell a person so swiftly. I'd have said gunshot but there'd been no sound. Mama was just laid out on the floor.

The snake began to grip onto my neck. Ella's science project was going to be a success after all.

I wanted to scream. I wanted to rip through my bonds. I wanted to beg.

But I was too frightened to do any of those things.

And that was when the United States Cavalry, in the fetching form of Kylie, came through the rear door.

Moving fast. Picking up the gun Mama had dropped.

Breaking into a run down the aisle right up to the altar and saying, "Put the snake back in the cage, Ella."

My heroine.

That same drugged dead response from Ella: "Be fun to try one of the serpents on a Jew."

Kylie pushed the gun in Ella's face. "Put the snake away, Ella, and then stand over there with your hands in the air."

"You can't order me around. Only God can."

The snake was still against my neck. I wasn't moving.

"Do it, Ella."

"You won't shoot me."

"You might be surprised."

"You probably never shot a gun in your life."

"You don't want to take that chance, Ella. Believe me."

And then she did it.

Wasn't it enough for my heroine to knock out Mama, grab the gun, and then rush the altar to confront the snake girl?

Not enough for Kylie.

She doubled-gripped the gun and fired it just to the side of Ella's head, the violent noise forcing Ella to jerk away, taking the snake she held with her.

Ella sort of windmilled backward for several feet and then fell off the side of the platform. The snake went flying off into the darkness.

Kylie came over and started untying me.

"How'd you knock out Mama?" I said.

"Rock. A big one."

"You saved my life."

She gave me a kiss, as she continued to untie my ropes.

"Yeah," she said, "and don't you forget it."

TWENTY-ONE

I'D NEVER REALLY BEEN to a "do" before. Picnics, I was used to. Family reunions, I was used to. Even union-sponsored hot dog-and-beer Democratic rallies in the park, I was used to.

But a real "do" such as you saw in the fantasy pages of *Playboy* or *Esquire,* with actual servants...all I could think of were the parties poor old Gatsby used to throw out on Long Island.

The Judge was wearing tennis whites and she looked damned good—tanned, trim, imperiously and regally beautiful. Not that she ever played tennis, you understand. Sweating, to her, was vulgar.

She just flitted around this golden glorious Midwestern afternoon—the temperature was in the high seventies and perfect—toting her glass of brandy and her Gauloise. A lot of her friends had come in from Chicago. You could tell they were big-city folks by the way they kissed each other on the cheek, the way movie stars do.

As for Milhous, well, the Secret Service basically imprisoned him. Wherever he was, they were, surrounding him. Only an esteemed few were let inside that fortress of heavily-armed bodies.

Kylie kept trying to hide. She whispered that she didn't have the right sort of clothes for an event like this, and didn't speak well enough to be in such august company, and hoped we didn't have to sit down and eat because she wasn't up on which fork and spoon to use at which point in the feast.

None of which mattered ultimately, anyway, because about five minutes before the feast was to be served on the long tables covered with starchy white tablecloths, the rain started.

And that was when I got my only really good look at Dick Nixon.

He was playing volleyball with a bunch of people.

Being summer, and being hot, and volleyball being a game that requires a lot of jumping and stretching, everybody but Dick was dressed in casual clothes, a lot of them, men as well as women, in walking shorts and golf shirts.

Not Nixon.

He was the only guy I'd ever seen play volleyball in a white dress shirt, necktie and wingtips. And I felt sorry for him. He didn't seem to even sense how strange and sad he looked—laughable and pathetic—volleyball played in suit and wingtips. But then I'd always felt sorry for him, sensing that I was as odd in my way as he was in his.

I never did actually meet him but as we rushed in the downpour from the elegantly dressed lawn to our car, I felt pretty sure for the first time that John Kennedy was going to win the election.

Playing volleyball in wingtips.

Poor old Milhous. After this election, I was pretty sure we'd never hear another political peep from him again.

ON THE WAY home, rain slapping and slamming my ragtop, Kylie said, "I'm really sorry the lovemaking wasn't so hot the other night."

"It was my fault, not yours."

"No, it was my fault. You're just being nice."

"C'mon, Kylie, it was just my Catholic guilt. Sleeping with a married woman. It inhibited me."

"You don't always have to be noble, McCain."

"I don't remember ever being noble."

"Well, sometimes you're sorta noble."

"Sorta noble—and on rare, rare occasions—that I'd accept."

"If I wasn't so hung up with Jewish guilt—I'm still a married woman—I don't think you would've been inhibited. It was up to me to free us both."

I reached over and took her hand. "There's only one thing to do."

"What?"

"Try again."

She smiled. And squeezed my hand. This was no kid-sister squeeze, either. "I think you're right."

"Try and try and try until we get it right."

"How about if we get a pizza and then go to your place and just watch TV for a while and kinda let things develop naturally."

"Great idea. But I have to ask you something. It's sort of kinky."

"Oh, God, McCain. I'm really not kinky at all. That was one thing Chad hated about me. No kinks."

"It's just this dream I've always had."

"This dream?"

"Well, this sexual fantasy, actually."

I had her going. I could see she was expecting to hear something so funky she'd throw herself out of the moving car.

"I have always," I said, "wanted to make love to a beautiful woman while I was wearing my wingtips."

"That's funny," she said. "I've always wanted to make love to a short, redheaded Irish guy while I was wearing my old Howdy Doody galoshes."

"Talk about compatibility."

"Yeah," she said. And then slugged me on the arm. "You are a true dip-shit, McCain. You know that?"

"Gee," I said. "I was hoping you wouldn't notice."

A FOREVER DEATH

Michael W. Sherer

Chicago sleuth Emerson Ward has to figure out who shot his friend, photographer Brady "Puppy" Barnes. Puppy had asked Ward to look into the case of some missing gems, stolen from his studio and replaced with fakes.

When Ward takes a part-time job at the ad agency that commissioned Puppy's project to photograph the gems, he uncovers a hornet's nest of suspects and more than a few motives for murder.

AN EMERSON WARD MYSTERY

"A slick narrative, quirky suspects, a fast-moving plot, and likable protagonist combine in this winner...."
—*Library Journal*

Available July 2003 at your favorite retail outlet.

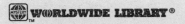

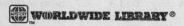

STEVE BREWER

dirty POOL

A BUBBA MABRY MYSTERY

Albuquerque P.I. Bubba Mabry's competition is William J. Pool, a Texas hotshot who asks Bubba if he wants some easy money. It's simple: drop off a large ransom payment to the kidnappers of a multimillionaire's son.

The money is picked up—by the young man himself, who quickly disappears. Now the rich father has a tantalizing new deal for Pool and Bubba: whoever finds his son first keeps the ransom money. *Nothing* will come between Bubba and $200,000—except murder.

> "...pure, clean fun."
> —*Albuquerque Journal*

Available July 2003 at your favorite retail outlet.

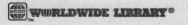